BLISSFULLY MARRIED

VICTORINE E. LIESKE

Victorine E. Lieske

PO Box 493

Scottsbluff, NE 69363-0493

www.victorinelieske.com

Created with Vellum

CHAPTER 1

Sidney's fingers flew across the computer keys as she held her breath and tried not to get her hopes up. A woman in her thirties sat in the chair opposite her desk, fidgeting with her acrylic nails. The late afternoon sun poured in the windows that faced the street.

Sidney smiled to put her potential client at ease. "Don't be nervous, Monica. I just have a few questions to ask."

Monica pasted on a weak smile. "That's fine. I'm just not used to doing anything like this. But Mia said you were the best, and I—well, I haven't had great luck picking out men to date." She twirled a strand of her dark hair.

"Most women who come in here are in the same boat. They want a committed relationship with a man who isn't…" She tried to think of a word that wasn't a put down.

"Weird?" Monica finished for her.

Sidney laughed. "I can understand why you'd say that." She straightened her suit jacket.

"I don't know what it is. I can't seem to meet a normal guy." Monica sighed. "I guess I attract the strange ones."

Sidney shook her head. "It's not you. Many women feel

the exact same way. Here at Blissfully Matched, we take your dating seriously."

Monica looked up. "We?"

Sidney swallowed. Why had she said that? Now she had to admit the truth. "Well, it's just me right now. But I'm very dedicated to finding a match for each one of my clients."

"How many clients have you successfully matched?"

"Six."

Monica blinked, and disappointment flitted into her eyes. "Only six?"

"Yes, well, that represents an eighty-five percent success rate." She wished she didn't have to count her sister, who had hired her to find Mr. Right but in reality just wanted more guys to string along.

The excitement seemed to drain out of Monica, like someone had pulled a plug. "I see." Her gaze flickered to Sidney's ring finger. "And what about you?"

And there it was. Her cheeks heated and she placed her hands on her lap under the desk. Maybe it was best to play dumb. "Me?"

Monica frowned. "Have *you* found your perfect match?"

Oh boy. This was where things always went downhill. Was it impolite to say, 'None of your business?' Sidney bit her bottom lip to keep the words from tumbling out. Instead, she shook her head.

Sidney's potential client was quickly becoming her lost client as Monica's frown deepened. "I see," she repeated. "And how much do you charge?"

This was not going well at all. She was supposed to talk up the service, get the client excited about it, build up confidence in her abilities, and then reveal her price structure. But she couldn't ignore a direct question. "You get up to ten matches for a thousand dollars."

Monica's eyes bulged and she stood. "Well, I'll need time

to think about it." Before the words were out, she was halfway to the door.

"Of course," Sidney called as she watched the woman bolt through the door and head down the street.

Great. Now how was she going to pay the rent? The business location she'd picked was perfect, right on the downtown strip with street parking outside her window. Lots of foot traffic. But the rent was tough to swallow. With a sigh, she closed the new client account she had started.

She was in trouble. And based on the report she'd run this morning, if she didn't land a client soon, she'd be kicked to the curb.

The door swished open again and her best friend strode in. Mia always looked like she was about to step out on a runway. Today she sported thigh high boots and a mini skirt. The getup would look ridiculous on Sidney, but somehow Mia pulled it off.

"Hey, girlfriend. How's business?" Mia took off her huge sunglasses and slid them into her clutch before plopping into the recently vacated client chair.

Sidney leaned back and let out a sigh. "Not good."

"What? I sent you three customers this week. Didn't any of them come in?"

"Yes." Sidney pressed her lips together and blinked away the moisture gathering behind her eyelids.

Mia softened. "What's wrong? They didn't hire you?"

"No." She looked down at the carpet. "I lost them when they found out I was single."

A deep frown crossed Mia's features. "What have I been telling you? You're the best matchmaker I know. Why don't you use those skills of yours to find *yourself* a man?"

Sidney fought the urge to snort. She was twenty-six. It wasn't like she was an old maid. "I don't need a man in order to succeed."

Mia rolled her eyes. "I'm not saying that, and you know it. You're smart. And funny. Men like you, but you push them all away. Maybe you should take your own advice once in a while."

A hollow feeling squeezed into Sidney's chest. The last thing she needed was another disastrous relationship. She'd sworn off men after the last one, Asher. Too good-looking for his own good. She'd thought they were on the road to engagement…a house in the suburbs…maybe two point five kids. Turns out he was on the road to Patty Mason. Her life had been a string of bad experiences with men, and she was through with it. "I'm fine on my own."

Mia gave her a pitying look. "Don't you think your customers would have more confidence in you if you had your own perfect match?"

She sighed. "Probably. But it's not fair." Having her own relationship had nothing to do with her ability to help others. But if no one would give her a chance, she might as well go back to waitressing. The hours stunk and it made her feet hurt, but what else could she do? She stared out the window. "I don't think I can do it. My heart can't take another horrible relationship."

A weird look came over Mia's face. "My Aunt Sylvia!"

Sidney stared at her friend and wondered about her mental state. "What?"

Mia hopped out of her chair. "Ha, I don't know why we haven't thought of it before. After her divorce, Aunt Sylvia couldn't go out without being hit on, so she decided to wear her wedding ring around. It worked. She could go out for the night and have no problems."

"Um…Okay."

"Don't you get it? You need a fake fiancé. A photo of a guy to put on your desk. A fake engagement ring on your finger.

Then people won't hesitate to hire you." Mia fluttered around the room like a little kid on a sugar high.

Sidney stood and rounded her desk, grasping Mia's arms. "Settle down. I can't lie to people. You're insane."

Mia grew serious. "Are you good at what you do?"

The question threw her off, and Sidney blinked. She *was* good at matchmaking. She loved searching for that perfect date for a client. She knew how to run background checks and what questions to ask to get to the heart of someone. And the thrill of seeing their eyes light up when they met was like nothing else. "Yeah, I am."

"And do you want to see your business die?"

A heaviness settled in her stomach. "No."

"Then isn't it better to give the appearance of success to your potential customers? It's like dressing for the right occasion. You're just adding a man as an accessory."

Sidney drew in a breath and let it out slowly. Maybe Mia was right. Maybe it wasn't like lying as much as it was having the right appearance. Like buying a nice pair of shoes. Only it was a man on her arm.

The look on her face must have told Mia she was considering it, because Mia pressed on. "If I find someone willing to play the part, will you at least think about it?"

Sidney laughed. "I can't believe I'm even talking to you about this."

"It's a good idea. You won't have to do much. Take some photos together and have one on your desk. You won't even have to really go out."

The insane idea might work. If she had a photo, and maybe a fake engagement ring, potential clients would probably not even ask about her relationship status. They'd just assume.

Mia pulled out her phone. "My brother's not busy today. Let me call him over."

"What? Now?"

Mia gave her that pitying look she always had when she thought Sidney was being too cautious and deliberate. "Yes, now. Look, if you change your mind, you don't have to keep the photos."

Before Sidney knew it, Ted had pulled into a parking spot and gotten out of his smart car. He was the total opposite of Mia. A computer tech, Ted embodied nerd like Shaquille O'Neal embodied athlete. He wore glasses and a button-up shirt, and every move he made was calculated. But he had a kryptonite, and that was Mia. When she said jump, he asked how high.

The door dinged as he walked in. He gave Sidney a sheepish smile. "Hey."

Sidney stood up from her computer chair. "Sorry to drag you over here."

"No problem." He pushed his glasses up with his index finger and rocked back on his heels. "I don't mind."

Mia grabbed his arm and pulled him toward the wall. "Come over here, Sidney. We'll take the photos where there's good light."

Mia pushed them together and made Ted put his arm around her. "Smile like you're in love."

Could she do anything more embarrassing? Sidney ignored the heat assaulting her cheeks and smiled so they could get this over with. After several poses and about a hundred clicks, Mia pronounced them done. She waved her phone. "I'll go get a few of these printed up."

Sidney faced Ted. "Thanks for doing this."

He ducked his head. "Sure." He stuffed his fists in his pockets. "See ya around."

After they left, Sidney sank into her chair and put her head on her desk, a feeling of dread sinking in. It had seemed like a good idea twenty minutes ago. Not so much anymore.

She forced herself to sit up and take in a cleansing breath. This was not a new low for her. It was a positive step in a proactive direction. Nice pair of shoes. That's all this was. She clicked to open a browser on her computer. Now all she needed to do was get a new customer.

Sidney spent an hour working her social media contacts and doing some soft advertising. When the door dinged and Mia waltzed back in, she was in a better mood. "Hey," Sidney said without looking up.

"Hey yourself. Look what I've got." Mia shoved a framed photo in front of Sidney's face.

The image of her and Ted smiling at each other actually looked good. Believable even. "Not bad."

Mia set the photo on her desk pointing toward the client's chair. She adjusted it a little, then smiled. "There. You're now in a happy relationship."

She grabbed Sidney's hand and slid a diamond ring on her finger. "And now you're happily engaged."

Sidney stared at the diamond on her hand. "Is this real? Where did you get this?"

Mia clapped her hands and bounced on her toes. "Isn't it perfect? It's totally fake but no one will know. It sparkles just like the real thing."

"How did you know my size?"

Mia laughed and raised an eyebrow. "Girl, we've been shopping together long enough. Don't you think I pay attention?"

Sidney stared down at the sparkling piece of jewelry. Another sense of dread settled in her gut, but she pushed it away. It was only a ring. And she didn't have to do anything else. Just wear it at work. That was it.

So why did she feel like she was making a big mistake?

CHAPTER 2

As the month progressed, the pressing dread lightened and the ring didn't feel as heavy on her finger. She had two clients sign up for her service and a third scheduled to come in on Friday. So far, no one had asked about her photo, so she hadn't had to outright lie. Things were looking up. She might even get to eat this weekend.

Her fingers clicked on the keyboard as the front door swung open and Mia rushed in. "I have the best idea!" She didn't wait for Sidney to speak. She went to the west wall and unrolled a long vinyl sign sporting the words: Blissfully Matched.

Sidney raised an eyebrow. "A wall vinyl?"

"Yes. I made one for your car as well. But that's not all. I think you should make this your success wall. Put up photos of all your successful matches."

"I only have six. And three of them were from before I went into business."

"That's okay, they still count." Mia's bangle bracelets clinked together. "We can put up several shots of each couple for now, so the wall looks full, and exchange them out as you make more matches. I brought some of my wedding photos to put up."

Sidney had convinced Mia to go out with Paul back in college. They were perfect for each other, and they'd both been having a difficult time in the dating pool. All it took was one date and they were hooked on each other. They married a year later.

"Sounds like a great idea."

Mia began prepping the wall for the vinyl. "This is going to look amazing."

"What font did you use? That looks stunning."

Mia answered, but something outside captured Sidney's attention and suddenly nothing else mattered. Someone stood on the sidewalk, squinting in her direction. A man who looked just like...Blake?

The bottom dropped out of her stomach and an incredible urge to hide overcame her.

Oh no. It couldn't be him. After all this time? What was he doing back in Bishop Falls? Had he seen her through the window? Good heavens, he was starting to come her way. Before her head could completely process what she was doing, Sidney slipped off her chair and dropped to the floor, crouching behind her desk.

Mia stopped talking mid-sentence. "Uh, Sidney? What are you doing?"

Her heart pounded in her chest, and she prayed that Blake hadn't seen her. Maybe he was looking into the sun, and it had blinded him. Yes, maybe that was it. He was squinting after all. "Dropped something."

The sound of the door dinging made her blood freeze. And then Mia cleared her throat. "Hello."

Blake's deep voice answered. "Hi. I'm sorry, I thought I saw someone through the glass. Is Sidney Reed in here?"

No, no, no. This wasn't happening. He couldn't be here.

And he couldn't find her crouching down behind her desk like some stupid coward. Sidney's ears grew hot and her legs cramped. She shook her head at Mia, giving her the 'no' sign, and prayed she would cover for her.

"Why, yes, she's here."

Mia was so dead. Deader than dead. Sidney was going to kill her, and then revive her just so she could kill her again.

There was no going back now. Her choice was to either stand up on her own and try to look dignified, or wait until Mia led Blake around the desk to find her squatting on the floor, chin deep in her own embarrassment. She peered under her desk for something she could use as an excuse. A silver paperclip lay in the dust and she snatched it, then stood, her neck now burning as well as her ears.

"Ah, I found it!" She held up the paperclip like it was proof that she wasn't insane.

"Sidney?" Blake cocked his head to the side, as if he was still not quite sure it was her.

She feigned innocence, tossing the paperclip on the desk. "Yes?"

A smile took over his features and he took a step toward her. "It's me, Blake."

It was him, all right. The same dark hair and piercing blue eyes, although he'd filled out over the last ten years. He was all man now. None of the boyish features remained. He had a strong jaw and muscular build. And he was here, in her matchmaking business, smiling at her. She blinked, pretending to be confused. "Blake?"

Behind him, Mia was completely freaking out, waving her hands and mouthing something she couldn't read. Probably something like, "Holy cow, he's totally hot!" At least, that's what Sidney was thinking.

Blake's grin widened. "Blake Wellington. We used to hang out as kids."

Hang out. More like, he would hang out with her older brother, and she'd tag along, ogling after him. But it was nice of him to act like she belonged. Sidney nodded and plastered on a smile of her own. "Of course. Blake. How have you been?"

Blake walked around the desk and enveloped Sidney in a crushing hug. It didn't last long, and he stepped back, appraising her with his gaze. "Look at you. All grown up."

His words reminded her of what he'd said the last time she saw him, and a sharp pain dug into her chest. She struggled to remain smiling. "Yes. All grown up." Her words came out clipped.

He just stood there, staring at her. Sidney motioned to Mia, to direct some attention away from herself. "Blake, this is Mia. Mia, Blake."

Blake shook Mia's hand in a polite gesture, but quickly turned back to Sidney. "How have you been?"

"Fine. What are you doing here?" The words slipped out before Sidney could stop herself.

"I just moved back. Got a job at Bishop Falls Memorial Clinic."

"You're a doctor?"

He nodded. "General practitioner."

So, he'd gotten his medical degree like he'd always planned. Good for him. She tried to swallow the hurt and embarrassment of the past and be happy for him. "That's nice."

He glanced around the small retail space she'd rented. "What is this? You own a business?"

Sidney nodded, feeling a sudden urge to prove to him that she was successful as well. "Yes."

He studied the sign Mia was preparing to put on the wall. "Blissfully Matched." Blake turned back to Sidney. "You run a dating service?"

The way he said it, with a lopsided grin like he thought it was a childish notion, made her stiffen. "No. It's a matchmaking service. There's a big difference."

He raised an eyebrow. "Really?"

Sidney bristled. What did he know about it, anyway? This wasn't any of his business. All the old pain came rushing in and she took a step back. "Yes. Really. And I'm actually quite busy right now, so if you don't mind." She motioned to the door.

If Blake was offended by her brush-off, he didn't show it. "I'm sorry for interrupting." He continued to smile, studying her. "I just can't believe you're..."

"All grown up," she finished for him, her stomach tightening. She needed to get away from him before she did something truly embarrassing. Like cram a stapler down his throat.

"Yeah." He shifted on his feet nervously. His gaze landed on the photo on her desk, then to her left hand. "You're married?"

"No," Mia said at the same time Sidney said, "Yes."

Blake cocked his head.

Sidney shot a death glare at Mia. It would have been simpler to say yes and make him leave. Now she was stuck. "I mean, no, but I will be. I'm engaged." She pointed to the photo. "To Ted."

Was it her imagination, or did his smile falter? "Congratulations."

There was an awkward pause when no one said anything, and Mia did a little dance behind Blake, trying to tell Sidney something but she had no clue what she was mouthing. When Blake turned his head she went back to fiddling with the wall vinyl.

"Um, well, nice to see you again, Blake." She thought

about shoving him toward the door, but stuck her hands behind her back instead.

To her dismay, instead of leaving, Blake took a step closer. "So, how does this service work? You keep a database or something?"

"It's much more personal than that," Mia said, answering for her.

How long would this torture last? She didn't want to think about Blake, her insane crush on him, and the most embarrassing moment of her life. But she also didn't want him to think her business was stupid. "I get to know each client, and I personally seek out the perfect person for them."

Blake scratched his chin, studying her. "Are you taking on new clients?"

Before Sidney could say no, Mia blurted out, "Yes. She is." She took his arm and led him to the desk. "Have a seat. Sidney will work her magic."

Great.

"And in fact, I have to run." Mia looked at her wrist, even though she had no watch. "Gotta go get that thing done. But you're in good hands with Sidney." Mia flashed a wide smile before backing out the door.

The room was suddenly too hot. Sidney waved her hand in front of her face and sat down. "Okay, then."

Blake settled back in his seat and got comfortable, like he didn't have a care in the world. Figures. He probably enjoyed her humiliation.

She opened her new client form and started rattling off the usual questions. After typing in his name, address, phone and email, she clicked to the more important part of the interview. "What are you looking for in a woman?"

Like she didn't know the answer to that. She might as well type Natalie in bold letters and be done with it. He'd always had eyes for her older sister. Why was he even in here?

"I want a woman who can think for herself. Someone not afraid to get her hands dirty. I love the outdoors so ideally she should too."

Ha. So Natalie was out. Sidney had always suspected his infatuation with her was all surface, no substance.

Blake continued. "She must make me laugh. And not be afraid to try new things. Snorkeling, hiking, canoeing, swimming…I'd like to do all of these with her."

Sidney typed everything he said. As kids, they'd done all those things together. He knew she loved them. She tried not to read anything into it.

"And do you have any physical preferences?"

His mouth twitched like it always did when he was trying not to smile. "No. I don't care what she looks like. I mean, pretty would be nice, but that's not important to me."

Sure. That's why he always drooled after Natalie. She swallowed the snort that was threatening to come up and typed, 'Must be shallow and drop-dead gorgeous.'

"Okay. Well, I think I have enough to go on." She stood. "I'll contact you soon with some options." She forced a smile.

He sat up straight and his mouth popped open. "That's it? I thought you said you get to know each client."

Blast. She had said that, hadn't she? Sidney cleared her throat while trying to decide what to say. "I…um…I already know you. So, no need."

Blake frowned. "We haven't spoken in ten years."

Guilt crept up, and she knew she couldn't treat him differently than her other clients. Just because she was embarrassed about the past didn't mean it was fair to take his money and push him off to the first woman who agreed to meet him. She shook her head. "Of course. This is just the beginning. I'll need to schedule another meeting with you.

Usually I take my clients out to coffee and we chat for a while. Does next week work for you?"

"I'm free tonight. Why don't I take you to dinner?"

Dinner? Like a date? Was he daft? "No, I couldn't." She pointedly flashed him her ring.

He glanced at her hand. "Just to talk. Complete my profile."

She normally didn't balk at taking a client out to dinner, but this was Blake. It had taken ten years to get over her crush on him. It was best to find him a match as quickly as possible and get far away from him.

Her hesitation must have given him courage. "I'm sure it will help you find my match." He gave her one of those devastatingly handsome smiles that made her heart pound.

She turned her gaze. Maybe going out tonight would give her the details she needed to find him a girl. Maybe the Band-Aid rip method was best. "Okay."

"Great. I'll go home and change. Where should I pick you up?"

She gave him her address. He stood and shook her hand. The instant their skin touched, electricity snaked up her arm and made her knees weak. She jerked her hand back and wiped it on her slacks. She must not allow herself to fall for Blake Wellington again.

Not if she wanted to keep her heart in one piece.

CHAPTER 3

As soon as Blake left, Sidney started to hyperventilate. Why had she agreed to take him on as a client? It was a bad idea. Just being around Blake brought up all those old feelings of hurt and embarrassment. The memory of that day, ten years ago, washed over her. It was the last time she'd seen Blake.

It had all started with a stupid, stupid dare.

~

Sidney plopped down on her bed and picked up her phone. Excitement shot through her as she dialed Leena's number. She turned up the radio, her favorite Savage Garden song playing. Leena answered on the first ring.

"You're never going to believe who's back in town."

"Blake?" Leena's voice shrieked over the line.

"Yes!" Sidney rolled over and hugged her pillow to her chest. "He's coming over for dinner tonight."

Leena screamed into the phone and Sidney pulled it away from her ear. "I know. I can hardly stay in my skin."

"This is it, Sidney. You have to tell him how you feel about him."

Sidney wrinkled her nose. "Are you crazy?" Sharing her secret crush with Leena was one thing. Telling Blake she'd been crushing on him for years was another. "I can't do that."

"Why not? How awesome would it be to have a boyfriend in college?" Leena squealed over the line and Sidney couldn't help but smile.

"I can't, Leena. I couldn't tell him."

"Then don't tell him. Show him."

"What do you mean?"

"You're sixteen now. You need to show him you're an adult. You're no longer that little girl that used to tag along after your brother."

Sidney's heart pounded. Leena was right. She was maturing. Blake always treated her like a little kid, but she wasn't a kid anymore. "How do I do that?"

"I'm coming over." The click told her Leena had hung up.

Fifteen minutes later, Leena arrived with a bag slung over her shoulder.

"What's that?" Sidney stepped back to let Leena into her room.

Leena unzipped the bag and pulled out a black dress and pair of high heels. "This is your secret weapon." She wiggled her eyebrows.

Sidney looked at the dress like it was a rattlesnake. "Uh, I don't think so."

"Come on. You never dress up. You've got to show him you're no longer the little Tom girl, climbing trees and skinning your knees and following after Grayson. You're a woman now." Leena held the dress up to Sidney's chest and whistled. "This will look great on you."

Sidney was hesitant. She liked her jeans and comfortable

T-shirts. She could be a woman wearing her normal clothes, couldn't she? "I don't know."

Leena made a face. "You coward."

"I am not!"

"I bet you're too scared to wear this dress."

Sidney grabbed the hanger. "I'm not scared."

"Then I dare you. I double dog dare you to wear this dress and some makeup."

The words rang in Sidney's mind. Maybe this was what she needed to do. Nothing else had worked. Blake was always nice to her, but never saw her as anything other than Grayson's little sister. Getting a makeover might be the thing to wake him up. "Okay."

Leena gloated, her smile wide. "Hurry, put this on. We've got a lot of work to do before Blake gets here."

A half hour later Sidney stared at herself in the mirror, her knees wobbling. She couldn't believe it was her. The transformation was amazing. She'd never worn makeup like this before. Leena had made up her eyes like someone in the movies, pretty blues and purples gracing her eyelids. Mascara helped her eyelashes pop, and cherry red lipstick made her lips full and inviting.

This was it. This was the day Blake would wake up and notice her. She felt empowered. She felt beautiful. Turning to Leena, she grinned. "I think I'm ready."

"You are gorgeous. He's going to fall all over himself. Just don't be afraid to flirt with him. Remember, you're showing him how you feel."

"Flirt?" A sudden unease washed over her. How was she going to flirt with him?

"You know, giggle at what he says. Look him in the eye, and maybe wink at him. Flip your hair over your shoulder. Stuff like that." Leena did the perfect hair flip and then smiled, blinking her eyes.

Flirt. She could do that, right? How hard could it be? Sidney squared her shoulders. "Sure." She shrugged. "I can flirt."

"And if all else fails, kiss him." Leena bounced up and down.

Sidney shook her head. "No, that's insane."

"I dare you."

Those words echoed in Sidney's head as she wobbled down the stairs in the ridiculous high heels Leena had made her wear. Kiss Blake? She mentally shook her head. No way. She'd just flirt with him and show him how she felt. That should work.

When she got to the dinner table, Blake was already seated next to Natalie, her older sister. Natalie was nineteen —a year younger than Blake—and attending the community college across town. Sidney slid into the seat across from Blake and smiled at him. She couldn't quite get up the nerve to bat her eyelashes.

Blake raised his eyebrows at her, but gave her a polite smile before turning back to Natalie. "How's school been so far?"

"Oh, you know." Natalie giggled and put her hand on Blake's arm. "Same old, same old."

Sidney stared at her sister. The viper was stealing her moves. Flirting. Heat crept up her neck and she sat up straighter in her chair. She wouldn't let Natalie ruin this night. "Yeah, Natalie's life is boring. If you want excitement, you should go to high school." She wiggled her eyebrows up and down in what she hoped was a sexy manner.

Both Blake and Grayson turned to stare at her, neither one speaking.

Her mother glanced at Sidney and gave her a funny look. She set a salad bowl on the table and sat down. "I think we're about ready to say grace."

As they ate, Grayson and Blake chatted about college life, and Natalie did her best to steal the show, giggling and flipping her hair just like Leena had done. Anger surged in Sidney, and she decided that two could play at this game. She let it all loose, flirting as hard as she could. She laughed louder than Natalie, batted her eyelashes more, and said whatever flirtatious things came into her head.

But no matter what she did, Blake always seemed to be looking at Natalie, a goofy smile on his face. She was being upstaged by her own sister.

When dinner ended, Sidney bolted up the stairs to her bedroom and sank down on her bed, not bothering to turn on the light. It hadn't worked. She'd gotten all dressed up, and Blake hadn't even noticed. She was wearing beautiful makeup, and still, Blake had barely even looked at her. What did she have to do?

Leena's words came back to her. "If all else fails, kiss him."

Footsteps sounded up the wooden staircase. Sidney flew to the doorway and peeked out. Blake was coming! Her heart pounded hard against her rib cage.

Kiss him.

Blake got to the top of the stairs and started down the hallway toward Grayson's room.

Kiss him. It echoed in her mind, over and over.

This was it. It was now or never. Sidney reached out and grabbed Blake's shirt and yanked him into her darkened bedroom. She threw her arms around his neck and drew his lips to hers.

At first he didn't respond. She'd probably stunned the poor guy. But she wasn't going to give up. She brushed her lips across his, reveling in the sweet and tender feeling. It didn't take long before he started to kiss her back. His arms wrapped around her waist and he pulled her closer. He took command of the kiss, his lips sending tingles through her.

She hadn't known exactly what to expect, this being her first kiss, and she wasn't prepared for the feelings Blake stirred in her. His lips were like velvet, softly caressing her skin. And then the kiss intensified. She ran her hands through his hair and he pressed her up against the wall.

Kissing Blake was like breathing fire, hot and dangerous, and yet she didn't want to stop. Her heart beat against his chest and her lungs ached for air, and yet she loved each and every sensation washing over her.

Blake pulled back, allowing her to gulp in air. He put his forehead against hers and moaned softly. "Oh, Natalie."

Sidney froze.

All the blood drained from her face, and she pushed Blake away. She flicked on the light, her knees about to give way. "What do you mean, *Natalie*?" She tried to catch her breath.

Blake stared at her, blinking, and slowly backing up. "Sidney?" His voice cracked.

Finally, Blake saw her for what she was. A woman. She gave him a tentative smile and smoothed her dress. "Yes?"

Blake ran a hand through his hair and swallowed. "What are you doing?"

That wasn't the reaction she had hoped for. A frown tugged her mouth down. "What do you think I'm doing?"

"I don't know, but you..." Blake took another step back. "You're just a little girl."

The words stung like a slap across her face, and she blinked back tears. It hadn't worked. He still saw her as a child.

Blake's face contorted into something she could only describe as disgust and he wiped his mouth. "You—I can't..."

"Stop." Sidney couldn't stand the humiliation any more. She turned her back on him and covered her face with her hands.

"Sidney." His voice had taken on a pleading tone.

He touched her shoulder but she shook him off. "Just go."

He hesitated for a minute before his footsteps echoed into the hall and down the stairs…and out of her life.

Sidney sank to her knees. What had she done?

CHAPTER 4

Blake flicked on his turn signal and changed lanes. Sidney Reed. He hadn't expected to see her still in Bishop Falls. And he hadn't expected her to be so...wow. He chastised himself for his thoughts. She was engaged. Off limits.

He slowed as he approached his turn. He hadn't thought of Sidney—of that kiss—for a long time. She'd been so young. He'd felt guilty for the way he'd kissed her. Thinking it was Natalie, he hadn't held back. It had been an amazing kiss. He hadn't realized a kiss could bring forth such strong feelings. But he never should have been kissing Sidney like that. He had been twenty years old, for Pete's sake. She was still in high school at the time. He'd been horrified when he found out he was lip locked with Grayson's kid sister.

Now she was an adult, and engaged. Why he'd signed up for her matchmaking service was beyond him. He'd had this insane urge to stick around, and just standing there would have been stupid. So he'd signed up. Dumb. But maybe some good would come from it. He did need to get out and find another woman. Stop licking his wounds from Melody and start on a new path.

He pulled into his driveway and clicked his garage door opener. He'd gone ahead and purchased a home in Bishop Falls. His mother's health had taken a turn for the worse, and he wanted to be close. This one-story bungalow was perfect for him.

The summer sun had spent the greater part of the day warming up his garage, and he was grateful for the air conditioning as he stepped into his kitchen. He was looking forward to tearing out all the old 70's laminate and putting in tile flooring and granite countertops. A good project was what he needed.

He tossed his keys on the counter and slipped out of his shoes. Thoughts of Sidney crept back into his mind. He'd better shower before their date tonight.

No, he couldn't think of it as a date. He had to place her firmly in the friend zone.

Bohemian Rhapsody played and he pulled his cell from his pocket and swiped the screen. "Hey, Ma."

His mother's soft voice came through the line. "Are you all settled in, hon?"

"Just about." He glanced at the pile of boxes still to be unpacked. "How have you been today?"

"I'm fine. Just tired."

"Do you need anything?" Now that he was closer, he could run something over to her if she needed it.

"No, sweetie, I'm good. Just wanted to check up on you."

Typical. She was so tired she could barely speak, but she called to see if he was doing okay. "Thanks. I just have a few things to put away."

"Have you heard from Melody?"

The familiar ache spread throughout his chest. "Not since the divorce settlement, Ma." That had been six months ago.

His mother was still hoping for reconciliation. Blake didn't want to disappoint her, but it was obviously over.

"You should call her."

He sighed. "All right." He didn't add, 'Once hell freezes over.'

"I just hate to see you alone."

"I know, Ma. Look, I gotta go. You call me if you need anything, okay?"

"I will."

"Love you." He hung up and stared at the wall. What could he say to her to make her understand? Melody had left him. There was no going back.

~

Metal hangers scraped as Sidney pushed through her wardrobe, searching for something to wear. She hadn't found anything the first three times, why did she think the perfect outfit would pop out now? Sighing, she settled on a blouse she'd purchased last month. It was red, which wasn't her favorite color, but it looked good with her dark hair and fit her nicely. She chose a pair of black slacks and comfortable yet dressy shoes. She didn't want to get too dressed up and send the wrong message.

After she dressed, she paced the living room floor, glancing out the window for Blake's car. This was just a client meeting. Not a date with Blake. She started repeating the mantra *not a date, not a date* in her mind until the knock on her door startled her. How had she missed him pulling up?

Her nerves jumped as she pulled the door open. Blake stood there looking like he'd walked off a photo shoot for men's casual wear. His blue button down shirt with rolled up sleeves looked perfect with his khaki pants. He raised one eyebrow, which probably meant something but all her brain would register was her mantra, which had turned into, *don't drool, don't drool.*

"Hi," she said, hoping her nervousness didn't show in her voice.

He smiled and held out his elbow, then seemed to think twice about it because he withdrew it and stepped back. "Where would you like to go?"

"It doesn't matter." As soon as the words left her mouth, she imagined sitting in a dark, romantic atmosphere and blurted, "How about Sue's?" Bright. Fun music. Lots of people. Perfect.

Blake seemed surprised at first, but quickly recovered. "Sure. After you." He motioned to a truck sitting in the parking lot, and Sidney took the lead.

Before he could open her door for her, she rushed ahead and climbed into the passenger seat. She didn't know why, but it felt like a triumph. He slid into the driver's seat and started the engine.

Sue's was a 1950's style diner with old-fashioned ice cream and the best hamburgers in town. Blake managed to get to the door first despite Sidney hopping out of the truck before he fully had it in park. He held the door for her and she covered a glare. Whatever. Still not a date.

"So, tell me about yourself," Blake asked after they sat down. "What have you been up to since high school?"

Ugh. Like she really wanted to talk about her pathetic life. "Went to college. Got a degree. Started a business. But we're not here to talk about me." She pulled a small notepad out of her purse. "Tell me what's been going on with you."

Blake fiddled with his menu, not meeting her eyes. "I guess I should tell you I've just gone through a rough divorce."

This was news to her. She'd tried to push all things Blake out of her life. She must have succeeded if she didn't even know he'd gotten married. "I'm sorry."

"It's okay." His face didn't look like it was okay. He swallowed hard. "It's in the past. I need to move on."

A heavy feeling settled in her chest. "If you're not ready to do this, we can wait—"

"No," he interrupted. "I'm ready. At least I want to be."

The server, dressed in a poodle skirt and saddle shoes, strode over to their table and took out her order pad. "What can I get for you tonight?"

Blake motioned for Sidney to go first.

"I'll have the cheeseburger meal, and can you substitute a vanilla malt for the soda?"

The server jotted something down on her pad. "Of course."

"I'll have the same." He folded his menu and handed it to the woman.

"You were always a chocolate shake fan."

He studied her, a slight smile on his face. "That was a long time ago. People change."

He was right about that. A lot had changed since they were kids. She nodded and handed over her menu as well.

"It'll be right out," the server said before disappearing into the crowd.

Blake sat there staring at her, so she picked up her pen. It was best to get this interview over with. "What brought you back to Bishop Falls?"

His eyes grew sad. "My mother's health isn't the best. I took a job here to be closer to her."

"I'm sorry to hear that." Blake's mother had struggled with her health for years. At one point when cancer was diagnosed, Sidney had thought she wouldn't make it, but she'd survived. Blake always said he wanted to be a doctor.

Sidney figured it was because of his mother. He wanted to fix her.

"It's okay."

Sidney wasn't sure how to lighten the conversation again. She stared down at her pad of paper.

"What about your parents?" he asked. "Are they still around here?"

She smiled. "Yes. They're still living in my childhood home. And Natalie's got an apartment over on Broadway."

His eyes lit up at the mention of Natalie. Great. Why did she bring up her sister? She might as well pair them up and be done with it. "In fact," she said. "I should set you up with her."

He raised his eyebrows. "Do you think Natalie would be a good match for me?"

The question threw her, and she stared at him. Since when did he care about that? He'd crushed on Natalie all through school. But of course, they were nothing alike. "Um…" What could she say that wasn't offensive? "Don't you want to go out with her?"

His lips pulled up in a half-smile. "Maybe she's changed, but when we were growing up, I'd invite her to go fishing with us, or bike riding. She always declined, saying she was more of an 'indoor girl,' as she put it."

"Right. But your eyes popped out of your head each time she walked into the room. I swear you left drool everywhere following after her."

He didn't deny it, and his laugh washed over her. "Your sister ran with the popular kids. She was a cheerleader. To a high school kid, she was the equivalent of a super model."

"You only liked her for her body?" She hissed, her voice low.

"I was seventeen."

She huffed. "You weren't seventeen when you thought

you were kissing her." The words flew out before she could stop them, and the instant they were out she wished them back. Why had she brought up her humiliation? Couldn't she have ignored that? Pretended it hadn't happened? She could have gone the whole rest of her life without saying that.

Blake's smile widened. "Twenty isn't far from seventeen."

"So you were a pig." Boy, the word vomit just kept coming, didn't it? Maybe if she kept going he'd drop the service and they'd be done.

"I was young. Immature. Now I'm looking for a serious relationship. I want someone who isn't afraid to experience life. I want someone who would be willing to..." His voice trailed off and he looked up. "Go skydiving with me."

She looked at him sideways. "Skydiving?"

"Sure, why not? It's fantastic. So freeing. There have to be adventurous women out there." His gaze traveled over her. "Like you."

"Me?" How had he gotten on the subject of her? "No."

"What? The twelve-year-old you would have jumped at the chance."

She took in a breath and let it out slowly. "The twelve-year-old me didn't have any inhibitions. I've changed a lot since then."

He squinted at her. "You seriously wouldn't go skydiving?" Throwing her a challenging stare, he paused. "Even on a dare?"

Oh no. Not the dare thing. "That might have worked on me when I was a little kid. But you hold no power over me now."

A wicked grin overtook his face. "Sidney Lane Reed," he said, and she rolled her eyes at the use of her full name. He used to blackmail her with it. She hadn't liked the fact that she was named after Grandpa Lane. However, she'd long since gotten over that. "I dare you to jump out of a plane."

She gave him a flat look. "No."

"I double dog dare you."

"What? Not the double dog dare. I'll have to do it now."

"Ha!" He smiled as if he'd won.

"I was kidding. Get over yourself. I'm not going skydiving just because you dare me. I'm not twelve."

Folding his arms across his chest, he huffed and leaned back in his chair. "You're no fun."

The server brought their food and Sidney took a big bite of her hamburger. She couldn't quite keep the smug smile off her face as she chewed.

"Maybe you need to go skydiving with me so you can gain experience in the kind of woman I'm looking for. That way, you can find me the perfect match."

She picked up a french fry. "Nice try." For some reason, the harder he pushed, the more she wanted to do it, if not for any other reason than to see the look on his face when she said yes. Plus, it might be kind of fun.

"It would help you get to know me better."

She smiled and dipped the fry into ketchup. "I'm getting to know you better right now."

He frowned. "Come on. What do I have to do? Beg?"

"You're just mad because you can't boss me around anymore. I no longer cater to your every whim."

He seemed to take that in. "Maybe." His gaze traveled over her, and he grinned. "Or maybe I just want to hear you scream as you fall a hundred and twenty miles per hour."

"Ha, like I'd scream." She probably would.

"Only one way to find out."

The urge to give in to him grew, and she stared down at her hands. Not a good idea to spend any more time with him. She could easily fall for him again. And it took a long time for her shattered heart to feel whole after the last time he broke it. She held up her hand. "Sorry. Engaged."

"Give me your phone," he said as he motioned. "I'll call Ted and make sure he's okay with it."

She sighed. No way was she having Blake call Ted. "Fine, I'll go with you. Ted won't mind."

It was Blake's turn for the smug smile. "Great. I'll get something scheduled."

CHAPTER 5

Blake had no idea why he had pushed Sidney into going skydiving with him. Maybe because when they were kids, Sidney would be the first to do something daring, but now she seemed to be…what was the word he was looking for? Timid?

Where was that adventurous attitude she used to have? Somewhere along the way she'd become cautious. He missed the old Sidney.

And maybe a part of him wanted to show off. He'd been skydiving since college and had gotten his instructor's license. He knew Sidney would love it—if she would give it a chance.

He picked up his malt and took a sip, studying the woman sitting opposite him. She glanced everywhere except at him. She was uncomfortable. Must be because of her fiancé. He didn't want her to feel like he was pursuing her. Best to get her talking about her business. "So, about your matchmaking service. Explain how it works, exactly."

"After answering all the questions, I hand select someone

to be your date. You get to meet them face to face. Think of me as your dating concierge. I look at more than what a computer would. If you feel sparks with someone, I put the service on hold for you while you feel out the new relationship."

"I see." He picked up a french fry. "And what if I don't like the match?"

"Your feedback is very important. We'll talk, and you'll tell me what you liked or didn't like about your match. With that information, I'll be able to fine-tune what you're looking for and we'll try again."

As she spoke she relaxed, and he was glad he'd changed the subject. Her smile seemed more genuine. She liked what she did for a living. That pleased him, for some reason.

After they finished their food and paid their bill, Sidney stared down at her note pad. "I still have quite a few questions. You got me talking about other things and I didn't get through them all."

"Why don't we head over to my place and we can finish them up?" The words were out before he realized how they sounded. She stiffened, and he quickly interjected. "I mean, unless you'd feel more comfortable staying in a public place. We could go to the park or something."

"The park will work fine." She scooped up her stuff and headed for the door so fast she was a blur. Why was she in such a hurry?

When they arrived at Pioneer Park, he was surprised when Sidney hopped out of the truck and started toward the old playground equipment. He was expecting to sit on a bench or maybe under a shade tree. He followed her to the sandy clearing. The sun had set, but it hadn't yet gotten dark. The sound of crickets filled the air.

She tossed her purse down and sat on a swing. "I haven't been here since we were kids. Remember when you were showing off and you jumped from the swing when it was super high?"

He chuckled as he sat on the swing next to her. "That was a new pair of jeans. My mom wasn't happy I ripped the seat out of them."

"You were so funny, clutching at your butt like that. I thought we were never going to stop laughing."

Her face lit up at the memory, and she laughed without inhibition. Sidney was always like that. Going forward without any reservations. It was what he liked best about her.

Still giggling, she took her note pad out and uncapped her pen. "What is the first thing people notice about you, besides your looks?"

He raised an eyebrow. "Are you saying I'm good-looking?"

"And cocky." She whacked his leg. "Be serious, or I'll match you to Big Bertha."

"The lunch lady? Is she still around here?"

Sidney laughed again. "I don't know, but you'd better behave or I'll find out."

"She's got to be in her sixties now," he said, trying not to laugh but failing.

"Another reason not to make me angry."

"Okay, fine. Um, I guess people are always telling me they like how I talk to anyone, no matter who they are."

She gave him a sideways look. "You *have* always been nice to everyone."

He shrugged. "I like people."

She scribbled something down on her pad. "Okay. What are your best life skills?"

"Man, you're down to the hard ones, aren't you?"

A grin stretched across her face. "You have to ask the tough questions to get to the heart of people."

"Okay. Well, I guess I'm good at time management."

She frowned, gripping the metal swing chain. "You might as well say 'I'm boring.' Think of something else."

"Boring? It's an important skill."

"Sure, for a job interview. Would you really want to date someone who thinks time management is most important?"

Point taken. It did sound dull. "All right, then. What would you put down?"

She pursed her lips in thought. "I would say, you have personal integrity. And the ability to laugh at yourself, as evidenced right here in this park." She giggled.

"You just won't let me live that down, will you?"

"It was the Spiderman underwear. You were, like, thirteen."

"I told you, it was laundry day." Her laughter prevented him from saying anything else. When she finally settled down, he said, "Why would you say personal integrity?"

She grew serious. "You've always had this great sense of right from wrong, and you're never afraid to speak up, even if it's not the popular thing. Like when you told Ricky Harms to take a flying leap when he was picking on Angela at school."

He studied her. She'd seen that? He hadn't thought anyone had noticed. Or cared.

"It's one thing I've always admired about you," she said, her voice quiet.

He didn't know what to say. "Thanks."

She went back to her paper. "What's something you can't live without?"

That was easy. "Classic rock."

"Ugh, not this *again*." She rolled her eyes. "You and your obsession."

"It's called *taste*."

"Well, your taste in music stinks."

He pushed her swing away from him, which just made it come back and collide with his. "You're so judgmental."

"Judgmental? Talk about the pot calling the kettle black. You're the one who won't listen to pop music, even though it borrows elements from classic rock."

"It hurts my ears."

She scoffed. "See? You're a music snob."

"And you probably listen to Justin Bieber."

"Oh, jump on the Bieber-hate bandwagon. That's original." She pushed off the sand to start swinging.

"So you do." He laughed when she stuck out her tongue at him.

He started his swing as well, even though his legs were too long and it was difficult not to hit the ground. She managed to swing higher, so he pumped harder. Soon they were in fierce competition.

"Finally, I can beat you at something," Sidney said as her swing rose a fraction of an inch higher, even though she was still gripping her notepad and pen.

"Only because of my long legs and manly bulk."

"Oh, how do you swing so high with that large head of yours?"

He laughed. "I'm just talented."

The cool evening breeze whipped through Blake's hair as they tried to outdo each other. His heart pounded and he felt like a teenager again. It wasn't just the swinging. It was…

He stopped his swing and hopped off, the realization hitting him. He started across the sand toward the bench. He couldn't feel like this toward Sidney. It wasn't right. He could not be attracted to an engaged woman.

Sidney called out to him. "You giving up?"

"Yep," he said without turning around.

She bounded off the swing and jogged over to him. "I

guess you admit defeat." She was smiling and trying to catch her breath, and he forced himself to look away.

"Yes. You beat me." He sat down on the bench, as close to the edge as he could get.

She joined him and gave him a sideways look but didn't say anything.

"Are you done with your questions?"

"Nope." She flipped to a new page and poised her pen. "What are you most passionate about?"

"My career. But that's a terrible thing to say on a dating questionnaire."

"You're right. Let's explore your answer." She squinted at him. "Why are you passionate about your career?"

He stared at the grass. "I want to help people. If I can make them healthy, and prolong life, I've not only helped them, I've done something for their whole family."

Sidney spoke as she wrote. "Saving lives."

He wrinkled his nose. "That sounds cheesy. I'm not superman."

"But that's what you love about being a doctor."

"I'm just a general practitioner. I'm not a brain surgeon."

"All right." She scribbled out the words on her pad and started writing again. "Helping people live healthier lives."

Blake slowly nodded. "I guess that's right."

"Okay. Just one more. What is your most important goal in life?"

He looked out at the setting sun. "I could say all kinds of things, like having a family, or being financially stable, but I think my most important goal is to live my life with no regrets."

She wrote on the paper. "That's a good one. Okay, we're all done."

Relief washed over him. Now he could take Sidney home

and stop feeling guilty for the way he was starting to look at her.

Maybe she would find him a match soon, and he could get Sidney out of his head.

CHAPTER 6

Sidney typed away at her keyboard, putting in the information she'd gathered the previous night. Blake was looking really good on paper. Too good. She had a ton of women in her database who would love to go out with him, and about a hundred of them matched up closely. The last part was finding someone with whom he'd have chemistry. He'd be in a solid relationship within a month.

So why didn't that make her happy?

She sighed and pushed away from the computer. Blake had waltzed back into her life yesterday, and her school-girl crush had picked up exactly where it left off—with her drooling and tripping all over herself when he was around. Why couldn't she get over that? What was wrong with her?

She needed to get him out of her head. If she matched him up quickly, she could push all thoughts of him away and move on. It was the only way to be rid of him for good. She clicked on the icon and scrolled through the matches the computer found.

Hannah Parsons. Too perky. She'd drive him nuts. Emma Thatcher. Too short. They'd look weird together. Chloe

Michaels. Now there was a possibility. Chloe was cute, but not too pretty. She was nice but not too sweet. And she liked classic rock music, and outdoor sports.

A sick feeling overcame Sidney. Chloe was perfect for Blake. She should make the call. Why was she hesitating?

She picked up the phone and stared at the buttons. One call. That's all she had to do. Taking a deep breath, she plunged ahead, punching in the number. Chloe answered on the third ring.

"Hey, Sidney, what's up? I haven't talked with you in forever."

"I know. This being an adult thing sure gets in the way of our fun."

Chloe laughed. "So, what's up?"

"I have a client looking for a relationship. I think he's a potential match for you."

"Ooh, what's he like?" Chloe's voice dripped with curiosity.

"He's athletic. An outdoorsy type. And he's got a good heart." Even though he's moody sometimes, she bit back, thinking of the way he'd hopped off the swing after she beat him.

"What does he do for a living?"

And this would seal the deal. "He's a doctor."

Chloe sucked in a breath. "Are you kidding me? Why isn't he already married? Is there something wrong with him?"

No. He's perfect. Sidney shook those thoughts away. "He's divorced. I don't know the details of the split, but I've known him for years. He's a good guy."

"Great!" Chloe sounded excited. "I'd love to meet him."

"Wonderful. Let me know your schedule and I'll set it up."

After she hung up, Sidney sat back in her chair and exhaled. There. She'd done it. Now Blake would be off the market and she could force herself to forget about him. Again.

~

Blake was surprised when he checked his phone and saw a message from Sidney. She'd already found him a match? Wow. She was fast. He set his lunch down on a table in the break room and punched in her number. "Hey, it's Blake."

She hesitated. "Hi."

She didn't say anything else, so he went ahead. "You said in your message that you found a match for me."

"Yes! Sorry, brain isn't working right now. I do have someone who would like to meet you. When are you free?"

"I'm free tonight."

Sidney mumbled something he couldn't quite hear. The phone rustled and then she came on. "Okay. I'll call Chloe. Anywhere in particular you'd like to meet?"

"Alfredo's."

"Oh, brother," she mumbled.

"What?"

"I said, 'That's perfect.'"

"No, you didn't. Do you have a problem with me taking her to Alfredo's?" He opened his milk carton and took a swig.

"It's…just a little cliché, right? Taking a woman to a fine Italian restaurant. It seems a bit…"

"Too romantic? Should we start out a little less formal? I don't want to seem overly eager."

"Yes. Somewhere casual is good."

He raked his brain to come up with some place that would work. "What about the mom and pop café over by Ben Franklin's? What's it called, The White Lilly?"

"That's fine. I'll give her a call. I'll text you if it works out."

Blake hung up the phone, and a light nervousness shot through him. Tonight he would go on his first date since the divorce. He had to remind himself that not all women were like Melody.

Oh, things had been great, at first. Weren't they always great in the beginning? Melody had seemed like the perfect woman. Unfortunately, he'd found out the truth about her. He took a bite out of his apple, pushing thoughts of his ex-wife out of his head. It would do no good thinking of her.

After work, Blake ran home to shower and get ready for his date. They were meeting at the café, taking some of the pressure off. Just a casual meet and greet. If he liked her, he could set up another date. If not, there wasn't even the awkward 'take her home' moment.

Blake arrived at The White Lilly ten minutes early, but when he mentioned he was waiting for his date, the greeter motioned to a woman sitting alone by the window. "I think your date is already here."

He took in her appearance before approaching. Her blonde hair was shoulder-length, and she wore casual clothes. Nice figure. Small frame. Light makeup, which was always a plus. Heavy makeup screamed 'high maintenance' to him.

Blake walked over to the table. "Chloe?"

She stood and stretched out her hand. "Hi, you must be Blake." Her smile widened as her gaze traveled over him.

They shook hands and he sat down across from her. An awkward silence stretched for a few seconds, so Blake blurted the first thing that came to mind. "You look nice."

"Thank you." She tugged at her collar. "I'm…a little nervous." She giggled. "I don't usually do this kind of thing, but when Sidney put a call out for singles, well, I decided it wouldn't hurt to put my information in her computer."

"So you know Sidney?"

Chloe nodded. "Yes, we had a class together in college, and we've been friends ever since. Nice girl. Unlucky in love, though." She clicked her tongue against her teeth.

He cocked his head to the side. "What do you mean?"

"Oh, you know, that whole Asher debacle. What a jerk."

The waitress interrupted them, handing them menus and taking their drink orders. After she left, his curiosity was too high to ignore. "What happened with Asher?"

Chloe's eyes widened in surprise. "You don't know? I thought Sidney said you guys were old friends."

"We are. I used to live up the street when we were kids, and was best friends with her brother. But I haven't seen her for years."

"Oh, well, Asher was her boyfriend. Looked like it was getting serious, too. He took her to a fancy restaurant for Valentine's Day and she thought he was going to propose. But instead, she found out he was cheating on her." Chloe flipped her hair over her shoulder.

Blake gaped. "He took her to a fancy restaurant to tell her about the other woman?"

"No. Sidney found out he had another date lined up for later that evening."

He winced. "Ouch."

"Yeah. Swore off men for good after that."

"You mean, until she met Ted."

Chloe's eyebrows pulled together in confusion. "Ted?"

"Her fiancé."

She slapped the table making a loud banging noise. "Get out! Sidney's engaged?"

He chuckled. "Yeah."

"When is she getting married?"

Blake hadn't asked. That was probably something important he should know. "I don't know."

"Ted...wait, isn't that Mia's brother?" Chloe picked up her water and took a sip.

He wasn't sure, so he shrugged. "Dark hair, glasses. Kind of skinny."

"Yes! That's Mia's older brother. Why didn't she tell me?" Before Blake had a chance to say anything, Chloe went on. "I guess I've been busy with work. We haven't really talked in ages. I'm going to have to call her."

This was bad. He'd been so curious, he'd let the conversation wander over to gossiping about Sidney. He should be getting to know his date. He cleared his throat. "So, Chloe, tell me about yourself. What kinds of things do you like to do?"

"I love tennis and golf. And I played football in high school. They let me on the boy's team. Actually," she said, leaning forward. "I kind of made a stink until they agreed."

Blake blinked. "Football?" He tried to reconcile the small woman in front of him with an image of a linebacker, and couldn't.

She laughed. "I know, everyone looks at me that way. But I was fast on the field and hard to tackle. And I loved it."

He chuckled. He liked her tenacity. "What about sky diving?"

She shook her head. "Oh, no. I'm afraid of heights."

A small disappointment sank in him, and he mentally crossed that off his list. No matter. The perfect woman didn't have to share all of his passions. "What do you do for a living?"

"I'm a dental assistant. I spend my day with my hands in people's mouths." She laughed.

"Well, I'm a general practitioner. My hands end up in all kinds of places you don't want to know about."

She laughed even louder and a few people turned to look at them. "What a pair we are," she said.

The waitress came to take their orders. Chloe pointed to her menu. "I'd like the Garden Burger, but hold the mushrooms, and can you use ground sirloin instead of hamburger? Oh, and lightly toast the bun, please."

The server hesitated. "I'll have to ask the cook about the hamburger."

Chloe frowned. "Never mind."

"Would you like anything to drink?"

"I'll take a raspberry lemonade, but go really light on the raspberry. And no ice." Chloe closed her menu.

The server scribbled on her pad. "Sure."

Blake ordered, and after the server left he said, "How long have you lived here in Bishop Falls?"

"I came here to go to college about seven years ago, and never left. I like the small town atmosphere, and with Omaha not too far away I have everything I need."

"That's one reason I like it here, too."

She placed her hands on her lap. "What's the other reason?"

"My mother lives here."

She hesitated. "You don't live with her, do you?"

For some reason, that question irked him. So what if he did? He had looked at moving in with her to help her around the house, but she'd insisted she was fine. "No."

"Good, because I dated *that* guy already and he was a disaster." She looked out the window.

Blake found himself counting down the minutes until the date would be over. It wasn't as if Chloe was bad company, she just didn't click with him like he'd hoped. The conversation turned strained. He knew she could feel it too, as they ate and tried to think of things to say.

After the meal, Blake paid the check and turned to Chloe. "Thank you for meeting with me."

"This is going to be our last date, isn't it?" She smiled, but it didn't last long.

"I'm sorry. I'm sure it's me."

"The old, it's me not you. I've heard that a million times." She touched his arm, and when there were no sparks, it confirmed his decision.

"It was nice to meet you."

"Thanks."

He wasn't sure what else to do, so he said good-bye and left. The evening sun had dipped along the tree line, and long shadows filled the parking lot. He hopped into his truck and started the engine.

Before he knew what he was doing, he found himself sitting outside Sidney's apartment. Why had he driven there? It was a Friday night. She probably wasn't even home. And yet, her lights were on, and her car sat in front of her apartment, the words 'Blissfully Matched' across the back window. Then he saw the curtain move.

Oh, busted.

Sidney came out the front door. "What are you doing here?"

She was wearing sweats and a T-shirt and he wondered why she wasn't out on a date with her fiancé. "Just wanted to talk, I guess."

She came over to the driver's side and leaned against the window. Even in her casual clothes she looked amazing. Her hair was pulled up into a messy bun, and it made his fingers itch to pull it down. He pushed that thought away. "How did the date go?" she asked.

He frowned. "Chloe was okay, but we didn't exactly mesh well."

"Oh." Sidney looked surprised. "What didn't you like about her?"

"There wasn't a lot, maybe a few little things."

"You've got to tell me so I can pick a better match for you next time."

"She was kind of picky about the food."

Sidney squinted up at him. "What do you mean?"

"She wanted the bun lightly toasted, and the meat substituted...stuff like that."

Sidney looked at him like he was being overly sensitive. "Okay." She dragged the word out.

"It wasn't just that, though." How could he explain it? "We didn't have any chemistry."

Sidney nodded. "I understand." She looked over at the setting sun. A light breeze carried her scent into his truck and he struggled to ignore it. He shouldn't have come here. His newly discovered feelings for Sidney needed to be caged. Swallowed. Buried.

"When are you getting married?" he blurted.

She stared at him. "Married?"

"To Ted. Your fiancé."

"Oh!" Pink colored her cheeks. "Sorry. Been a long day." She tugged at her ear lobe. "We haven't set a date yet." She wouldn't look him in the eye.

"Are you and Ted...having problems?" Guilt crept in. He should keep his nose out of her business.

"No." She bit her lip, which made him question her answer.

"If you need to talk..." He let the invitation drift off. What was he doing? That was inappropriate. He should let her and Ted work through things together.

She looked him in the eye, pausing. "Thank you," she said, her voice almost a whisper. She took a step away. "I'd better..." She motioned toward the door.

"Yes. Okay. See you later." He backed up his truck and pulled out of the parking lot, forcing himself to keep his eyes in front of him and not glance back at her.

CHAPTER 7

Blake had a hard time sleeping, and after an hour of tossing and turning, he finally got up at five o'clock. Why couldn't he get Sidney out of his head? She was taken, and there wasn't anything he could do about it. Or rather, should do about it. If she were having trouble with her fiancé, he had to butt out of it.

His pent-up energy had him crawling out of his skin. In a moment of frustration, he decided this was the perfect time to tear out that useless kitchen wall. It wasn't load bearing, and there was no real purpose for it. After cutting through the drywall with his utility knife and making sure there was no electricity, he grabbed his sledgehammer and slammed it into the wall. A satisfying hole punched through, and he repeated the process, making the hole bigger.

He ignored the mess as he worked, enjoying the sight of the wall opening up. He pounded out the drywall and carried large chunks of it to the garbage. Then he worked on removing the studs with his saw. By the time he was done, his muscles ached, but he was glad for the distraction. He hadn't thought about Sidney for the last three hours.

A hot shower sounded good, so he put his impromptu renovations on hold and entered the bathroom. As the soapy water cascaded down around him, the answer came to him. He had to call Sidney and quit her service. He'd pay her full price. It wasn't fair to back out of the contract. He just needed to get away from her. It was a large enough town that he'd probably only bump into her if he went out of his way to. He could stay away. Let her work things out. It was for the best.

After he dressed, he ran to the store to get some much needed grocery items. He had finished his milk yesterday, and he was out of fruit and bread. As he wheeled his cart down the aisle, he spotted Sidney's friend looking over the bananas.

"Hi. Mia, isn't it?"

Mia glanced up at him, then smiled. "Hey, you're Sidney's old friend." She did a quick full-body appraisal of him, her smile widening. "How are you?"

He smiled politely. "Fine."

Mia was wearing a bright shirt with a Japanese print, a tight skirt and platform shoes. She nudged him. "How's it going with Sidney?"

"What?" Why would she ask that?

Mia set the bananas she'd been examining in her cart. "You just looked like you were hitting it off, that's all."

He narrowed his eyes at her. "Isn't Sidney engaged? To your brother?"

Mia paused for a second, her cheeks coloring. "Oh. That. Um…"

"What?" Had they broken up?

A guilty look colored her face. "I really shouldn't say anything."

He folded his arms across his chest. "Are she and Ted breaking up?"

Mia shook her head, but kept her lips tight.

What was going on? Why was Mia acting this way? The clues started to fall into place. Sidney home on a Friday night. Chloe not knowing Sidney was engaged. Mia acting weird. "She's not really engaged, is she."

Mia waved her hand and looked around. "Hush," she said, her voice low.

He stared at her, but she didn't say anything else. "Well?"

"Okay. You're right. She's not. It's all a ruse, to help with business."

The shock of the truth reeled through him. "Why would she lie?"

Mia bit her lip. "We made up the engagement because her clients were having trouble putting trust in her abilities. It didn't seem plausible that she would be able to match others when she herself was single."

"Why didn't she tell me?"

A sudden panic crossed Mia's face, and she gripped her shopping cart. "You can't tell her I spoiled it. She'd kill me, and you don't want to have blood on your hands, do you?"

Despite his surprise, he chuckled. "No, I wouldn't want that. But I don't understand. She had plenty of opportunities to come clean. Why would she go on pretending? We've known each other forever."

Mia shrugged. "Sidney keeps saying she doesn't need a man in order to be successful."

Blake let her words sink in. Maybe Sidney wanted to stabilize her business before seeking a relationship of her own. Whatever the reason, the heaviness that had been pressing down on him all morning lifted.

Sidney was single.

"Thanks, Mia." He could have kissed her, but settled on a handshake. "You're the best."

Blake left her standing in the fruit section, staring after

him. A plan was already forming in his mind. He had to see Sidney. Make her admit the truth to him. But first he needed to pack a picnic lunch.

~

Sidney pulled out a bowl and her favorite morning cereal and crossed the kitchen tile to get the milk. Her pink bunny slippers made a slapping noise as she walked. There wasn't anything better than a lazy Saturday morning—eating breakfast in your pajamas and getting on Facebook to see what funny memes people were sharing. Maybe she'd read some more of that book she'd started last night.

Just as she finished her cereal, the doorbell rang and Sidney sighed. Probably some neighborhood kid selling something for a school fundraiser. That was pretty much all she got these days. Well, if it was doughnuts again, she'd be all over that.

She swung open the door and froze. Blake! She yelped and slammed the door in his face, her heart pounding. She was in her pajamas! And she hadn't even looked in the mirror. Her hair must look atrocious.

A knock sounded and she opened the door a crack. "What are you doing here?"

Blake coughed into his fist. He stood there, trying not to grin but failing miserably. "Just wanted to see you in your bunny slippers."

"Very funny. I just got out of bed."

"I can tell." His lips twitched.

"Go away." She started to close the door but he stopped it.

"Wait." He grew serious. "I wanted to apologize. I don't want to get in the way of you and...*Ted*."

"Thank you. I appreciate that." Again she tried to close the door, and again he wouldn't let her.

"I'm heading out today. Thought I'd go over to Blue Oak Lake and rent a canoe."

The mention of canoeing brought back memories of them as kids. "Sounds fun. Have a great time." The door wouldn't budge. She looked down. The jerk had his foot wedged in it.

"I thought maybe you and *Ted* would like to come."

He had a funny look on his face and she narrowed her eyes at him. "Why are you acting like this? And why are you saying Ted's name like that? What's up?"

Scratching his chin, he said, "Nothing. Just thought you'd like to enjoy the nice day."

"Well, sorry. Ted is out of town, and I've got stuff to do."

He peeked past her into her apartment. "Like what?"

"Stuff!" She didn't say that stuff involved reclining on the couch and reading.

"Can't it wait?" he practically whined. "I want to see if you tip the canoe like last time."

"That was *not* my fault." She tried to say it indignantly, but her smile ruined it as she pictured Blake climbing out of the lake and tipping his shoes upside down to let the water run out. She had laughed so hard.

"Prove it. Come with me."

"You're such a child!" She let out a very unladylike grunt. "Fine. I'll go with you." She had to admit, canoeing with Blake sounded like an awesome way to spend the day.

"Great." Blake pushed the door open and walked in.

She glared at him. "Come on in and make yourself at home."

He plopped down on the sofa and put his feet up on the coffee table. "I will."

"Ugh," she muttered under her breath, but couldn't force

the smile off her lips. "At least take off your shoes. The hardwood floors are new."

He slipped his shoes off and picked up her romance novel, reading the back while waving her away.

"I'll just go shower and get ready then."

She snuck into the kitchen, rinsed her bowl and placed it in the sink. Then she gathered her clothes and locked herself in the bathroom. Why was her heart pounding? It was just Blake. It wasn't like he was asking her on a date or anything. He had invited her and Ted.

As she passed the mirror she gasped. Her hair was sticking up at all angles, and the eyeliner she forgot to wash off yesterday made her look like a raccoon. Thank goodness Blake thought she was engaged to someone else. There was no way he'd be interested in her after seeing her like that.

She quickly showered and made herself look presentable. Pulling her hair into a ponytail, she eyed her reflection. Not bad. A marked improvement. A quick spray with her favorite fragrance and she deemed herself ready.

When she exited the bathroom, Blake was in the kitchen snooping. He held up the box of cereal she'd forgotten to put away. "Cap'n Crunch? Really?"

She swiped the box away from him. "Don't you talk. You drank chocolate milk for lunch every day in high school. I'm pretty sure that means you can't make fun of my choice of breakfast cereal."

"Who wants plain milk when there's chocolate?"

"And who wants Cheerios when you can have Cap'n Crunch?" She opened the cupboard and shoved the box inside. "So, are we going to argue about cereal or are we going to the lake?"

Blake motioned toward the front door. "After you."

Once they were in his truck and on the road, Sidney

reached over and switched on the radio, then turned the dial to her favorite pop station. Blake groaned. "Seriously?"

"You need a little more culture."

He laughed. "Pop music is not *culture.*"

"Of course it is. Just relax. It's not going to kill you." She turned up the Demi Lovato song and started singing along. Warm air whipped her hair as she rolled down her window.

Blake changed lanes. "Why do you always do that?"

"What?"

"Roll down your window when we're on the highway. The wind noise makes it impossible to talk."

She put her hand to her ear. "What? I can't hear you."

He made a face. "Very funny."

She turned the radio up louder and sat back in her seat, somehow satisfied. "The breeze is nice." With her hand out the window, she let the force of the air move it up and down, depending on what direction she twisted it.

"You're just like a little kid."

The words stung, but she didn't let her face show it. "Am not." It was a terribly immature thing to say, but she didn't care. If he still thought of her as a little kid, then fine. It wasn't as if they were going to be a couple anyway. Maybe it was best if he thought of her as a child. Took the pressure off her.

They rode in silence the rest of the way to the lake. After they rented the canoe, put on their life jackets, and got the canoe ready, Blake ran back to the truck and grabbed a large paper sack.

She eyed him suspiciously. "What's that?"

"Picnic lunch."

Folding her arms across her chest, she frowned. "How did you know I was going to agree to go canoeing with you?"

He grinned. "I'm just a good guesser."

"You're a manipulative little—"

Blake stepped forward and put his finger on her mouth, halting her words. "Don't say anything you'll regret later."

He stood there, dangerously close to her, his finger touching her lips, while her heart pounded in her chest. All thought left her head, and the only thing she was aware of was his masculine soapy scent and the feel of his warm skin on her lips.

Then he removed his hand and took a step back. "Let's get in."

CHAPTER 8

Blake dragged his oar through the water, feeling the burn in his muscles. The warm sun beat down on his back. Sidney sat in front with her back to him, her hair blowing in the breeze. The weather was perfect for this.

Getting her to admit to the ruse was proving harder than he'd thought. When he'd make comments about Ted, he'd figured she'd sigh and come clean. Not so. She was holding onto the lie like a white-knuckled child holding a lollipop.

He quickly abandoned the idea of forcing it. He didn't want her confessing because she'd figured out he already knew. His tactics changed. He decided to lay off and take it easy. See if she would tell him the truth on her own. Maybe she just needed to feel more comfortable around him.

"I forgot how relaxing this can be." Sidney smiled at him over her shoulder, her muscles straining as she worked her oar.

Blake took a moment to study her. Her brown hair shone in the sun and she practically glowed as her smile took over her face. He'd never seen anyone lovelier.

She slapped her oar in the water and splashed him. “Slacker.”

He chuckled and his cheeks heated when he realized he’d stopped paddling and was staring at her. He joined in her rhythm with his oar. “I think we’re almost there.”

“Wow.” Sidney glanced to her side at the shade trees lining the bank. “Used to take a lot longer to get here.”

He flexed his arm. “What can I say? I’ve filled out.”

She snorted and rolled her eyes, but a smile curled up the corners of her mouth. She eyed the grocery sack. “What did you bring?”

“Peanut-butter-jelly-and-marshmallow sandwiches.”

Her laugh rang out. “You did not.”

“You’re right. I figure your tastes have changed since you were six.”

“Grayson is to blame for that one. He told me that was how all the rich people ate peanut butter and jelly, and I believed him.”

“Really?” He raised an eyebrow.

“Yes. I figured he knew what he was talking about, being ten and all. Never stopped to think about the complete lack of galas in his life.”

“Big brothers know everything.”

The canoe made a noise as the bottom scraped the sand in the shallow water. Blake set the oar down and swung his foot over the edge of the boat so he could stand without tipping it. He stood, grabbing the grocery bag. Sidney hopped out and walked up the bank. He followed her under the shade tree. She took the sack from him and peeked inside.

“I just threw together some ham sandwiches.”

“And you made potato salad?” She lifted the container out.

“Store bought. Sorry.”

"That's okay. I've been craving it and haven't had any this summer."

He sat on the grass and she plopped down beside him. She took out the sandwiches and paper plates he'd stuck in the bottom and handed him a plastic fork.

As they ate, the mood turned more serious. Sidney looked like she was going to say something several times, but stopped herself. Finally, she said, "How long were you married?"

That wasn't what he expected, and he blinked. "Two years."

She lowered her gaze. "I'm sorry things didn't work out."

"They were working out fine for me. I had no idea anything was wrong until I came home one night and Melody was packing."

Sidney gaped at him. "Seriously? That's awful. You'd think if she was unhappy, she'd at least try to talk about it."

The familiar ache in his chest started up. "I thought she married me because she loved me. Turns out, she loved the idea of being married to a doctor. Only, I was in residency and had loads of student loan debt. I guess I wasn't giving her the life she'd always imagined."

"She left you because you weren't making enough money?" The shock on her face was evident.

He stared out at the gentle waves on the lake. "Apparently she was willing to wait for the money—until she found someone else who already had it. Some big shot who'd inherited a few million dollars. Melody said it wasn't personal. Like it was a business transaction."

His stomach soured at the memory.

"Oh, that's terrible." Sidney stared at her sandwich. "I'm sorry."

He picked up his Coke and unscrewed the cap. "It was

better to find out two years into the marriage, instead of twenty."

She nodded, looking up at him. "You said the divorce was rough. Did she get a lot in the divorce settlement?"

"No. We'd not been married long, and we had no children." He let out a mirthless chuckle. "She was livid that they denied her alimony. Her face turned purple when the judge told her to go get a job."

Sidney laughed. "I bet that was priceless."

He sobered. "Taught me a lesson. Not everyone in this world has good intentions."

She looked away. "Yeah. Don't I know it."

He wondered if she would elaborate, but the silence stretched out between them until they'd finished eating. He started packing up the things, the thought of someone hurting Sidney making his gut feel tight. Maybe that was why she wanted to wear the fake ring. He understood the instinct to shield yourself from any more pain.

Sidney slid the dirty paper plates into the trash sack he'd brought and tied the top. "Thanks for bringing lunch."

"Sure." The mood was heavy and he didn't know how to lighten it back up again. "Should we…" He motioned to the canoe.

"Yes." She started down the small embankment to the water. After they were situated in the canoe, they began maneuvering out of the small area near the shore. Together, they paddled in silence as the canoe cut through the water, crossing the lake.

~

Sidney silently beat herself up. What had she been thinking, asking him about his divorce? Why would she want to kill the good mood like that? Now Blake sat behind her, a stony expression on his face as he pulled his oar through the water.

She should have known better. Who wanted to talk about their ex? She certainly didn't. She bit her lip, trying to decide what to say. "Listen, I'm sorry I—"

"It's okay," he said. "No need to apologize." He smiled, but it didn't last.

"I really shouldn't have pried. It's none of my business."

He cocked his head to the side. "We're friends. Talking about the hard stuff is part of it."

Friends. She liked the sound of that. She'd never been on that level with Blake before. She'd always felt like the little sister who tagged along. Grayson sometimes complained about her, but Blake would shrug and say, 'She's cool.'

"Yeah, I guess," she said as she squinted from the reflection of the sun on the water.

"I'm sure you've had your share of heartbreaks." Blake stopped paddling.

What did he mean by that? Did he know about Asher? Was he trying to get her to open up about it? She frowned. She didn't want to talk about it. "Just like everyone. Hey, remember when we decided to explore that cave, and you freaked out?" She glanced behind her.

He laughed, the lines around his eyes crinkling. "I haven't thought of that in years."

"I thought you were going to have an aneurism, waving your arms in the air."

"There was a bat!"

"That was Grayson, messing with you!" She laughed.

"You're kidding me. All this time I thought a bat had nearly taken off my head."

"You're so gullible."

They continued to paddle in companionable silence until

they'd reached the other side of the lake. Blake wiped his forehead. "I guess we should be heading back."

She nodded. "Okay."

By the time they got back to the dock, her muscles ached from the exertion and she was ready for the break. After stopping the boat, Blake stood and extended his hand to help her out. She clasped it and took a step. The canoe rocked and caught her off balance. She yelped and grabbed ahold of him.

He caught her, his strong arms holding her steady. "Whoa. Watch out, or you'll end up in the lake."

She blinked up at him, her heart racing from the close proximity. Man, he smelled good. Like fresh out of the shower mixed with date night musk. She splayed her hand over his chest with the intention of pushing him away, but the feel of his muscles under her fingers mesmerized her and she stood there staring at him. If she tilted her head a little, their lips would meet. She could relive that kiss from so long ago. "No," she mumbled.

"No?"

She shook her head to clear it. "I mean thanks." She squirmed away from him and scampered out of the canoe.

What in the world was that all about? What was wrong with her? So Blake had muscles. And rock hard abs. Big deal. Why had she gone all butter brained? Stupid crush.

She helped Blake with the picnic sack as he climbed out, and they headed back to his truck. By the time they pulled out onto the highway, her heart had normalized.

Blake turned to her. "You all right?"

"Fine," she said a little too quickly. Arg. Why couldn't she just act normal?

"You got quiet all of a sudden."

Great. What was she supposed to say, 'My childhood crush took over my brain for a moment and I couldn't stop thinking about kissing you?' Not likely. "I'm not quiet. Just content."

He looked like he was trying not to smile. "Content, huh?"

"I mean, it's such a nice day out. And the lake was calming. That's all."

"I see." He smirked as he drove, as if he knew a secret.

She wanted to smack that smug grin off his face but folded her hands into her lap instead. They were silent on the drive home. When he pulled up to her apartment, she saw a little red Toyota with a smiley face antenna topper sitting in the parking lot.

Natalie.

Dang. Why had she given her sister a key? She never used it for emergencies. She was probably in there eating Sidney's Cracker Jacks and watching Netflix, the moocher.

"Well, thanks for the picnic. See ya." She hopped out of the truck, hoping he'd just go away.

Unfortunately, he turned the truck off and got out. "What do you have planned for dinner?"

Just as the words left his mouth, Natalie came waltzing out of the apartment. "Blake? Is that you?"

Of course Natalie looked like she'd stepped out of a television show, her little daisy duke shorts and tight top showing off her fabulous figure. He did a double take. "Natalie?"

"Oh my gosh, I heard you were back in town." She ran over to him and hugged him. "How are you?" She smiled at him.

Sidney ground her teeth. Little Miss Flirtatious was working her magic.

CHAPTER 9

Blake pulled back from Natalie. She sure hadn't changed much from the last time he'd seen her. "I'm fine. How are things going for you?"

Natalie combed her fingers through her hair and smiled, her lashes lowered. "I'm good. Real good. We should get together." She almost purred when she spoke.

"Well, I was just about to..." He glanced at Sidney and froze. She stood there, her mouth in a straight line, arms folded tight across her chest. Had he stepped into a family feud? He coughed. "Um, I was..."

Natalie grabbed his arm and saddled up beside him. "Come inside. We should catch up."

Before he knew it, she was dragging him into the apartment. Sidney followed behind them, making sure they removed their shoes. "What are you doing here, Natalie?"

"I heard there was a *doctor* in town."

Oh brother. He wiggled out of her grasp and took a few steps back. Just what he needed. Another woman like his ex, more interested in his profession than him.

Sidney's face blanched, and she looked like she wanted to slap her sister. "Nat, where's Gregg?"

Natalie's expression soured and she looked at her fingernails. "We broke up."

"Aw, I'm sorry." Sidney's face betrayed her lie. "Sit down. You must be upset. I'll bring you a Diet Coke." She turned to him. "Do you want a soda?"

"Sure. Thanks."

Natalie plopped down on the couch and Blake took the opportunity to snag the accent chair. "How long were you dating Gregg?"

"Two weeks." Natalie looked bored. "But that doesn't matter. What have you been up to?" She leaned closer.

"Just getting everything unpacked."

She grinned. "If you need any help—"

"No, thank you." He could imagine what kind of help Natalie would be.

"Moving is hard." She sighed dramatically. "But it's nice to already know people here."

He nodded, unsure of what else to say to her.

She squinted at him. "You've got something on your..." She pointed to her face.

He wiped his face, but didn't feel anything.

"No, you didn't get it." She got up and sashayed over to him. Before he knew what to do, she was sitting on his lap. She crossed her legs and ran her finger across his lips.

"There."

Stunned, Blake just sat there.

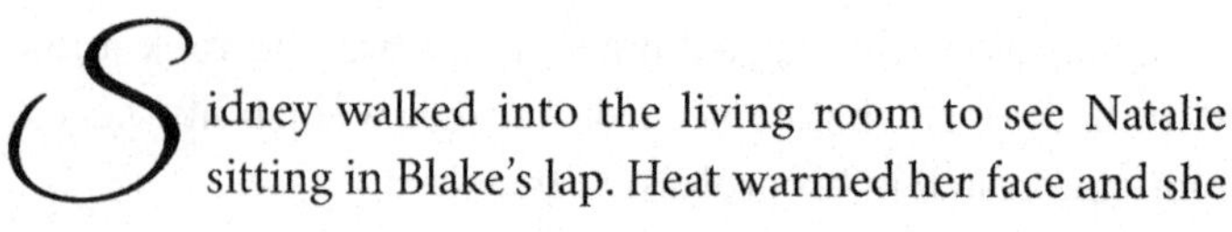

Sidney walked into the living room to see Natalie sitting in Blake's lap. Heat warmed her face and she was about to clear her throat when Natalie laughed and said, “Do you remember when you kissed me behind the trees in our backyard?”

The drinks in her hands slipped and fell to the hardwood floor. She watched in horror as Coke, ice, and shards of glass flew everywhere. Blake jumped out of his chair so fast that Natalie bounced off and landed on her butt.

He took a step towards Sidney. “Are you okay?” Before she had a chance to answer, he said, “Don’t move. There’s glass everywhere. I’ll go get a broom.”

He tiptoed like Dick Van Dyke doing one of his Mary Poppins dances as he tried to avoid the glass and get into the kitchen. Sidney stared at her sister, speechless. It suddenly made sense why Blake had kissed Sidney so passionately that day. Why he’d called her Natalie. They’d been kissing in the shadows all along. The old hollow feeling worked its way into her chest, but with a new humiliation attached to it.

Blake called from the other room. “Where’s your broom?”

She sighed, unable to do anything but just stand there. “The closet by the back door.”

He came into the room and started sweeping the mess into the dustbin. When the glass had been contained, Sidney walked through the kitchen to get the mop. She filled a bucket with water and squirted some floor cleaner in.

Blake took the mop from her. “Here, let me.”

“Fine.” She brushed past him, irrational anger making her shake. She stalked into her bedroom and pulled off her socks, now dripping with soda. How could she have been so stupid? It had been obvious. Blake had always liked Natalie. That was no secret. Dumb of her not to realize Blake had been kissing Natalie all along.

Idiot.

And now here he was, back to flirting with Natalie. And

he'd said he didn't want to be with her, which made it ten times worse. He had no intention of getting serious. He was just playing the flirt. What a jerk.

She shoved her feet into clean socks and walked back into the living room. Blake wrung the mop into the bucket and turned to her. "All cleaned up."

Natalie was sitting on the couch, a pout on her face.

"Thanks." Sidney took the mop from him and went to rinse it out. She twisted on the faucet and let it run.

"Hey."

She turned to bump into the solid wall of Blake's chest. Geesh, what was he doing, trying to give her a heart attack? Her heart thumped against her ribcage as if it wanted out.

He held up the bucket. "Can I dump this in here?"

"Better dump it in the toilet."

He paused, staring at her for some insane reason. Why did his gaze make her feel all wobbly inside? "Down the hall?" he asked.

She nodded.

He left and she could finally breathe. What was wrong with her? Why did her crush on him suffocate her like that? It was dumb. He and Natalie had obviously picked up right where they left off. She needed to get them out of her apartment.

She put away the mop and went to talk to Natalie. Her sister approached her as she entered the living room. "We should make Blake a welcome home dinner." She was back to her coy self.

"Actually, I have something I need to do." She waited for her sister to move, but when she didn't, Sidney said, "So... goodbye." She motioned toward the door.

Natalie huffed. "Fine. But I'm calling you later, and you're going to spill it."

"What are you talking about?"

"You and the good doctor. I want to know what's going on." She grabbed her purse and slipped on her shoes, then walked out the door.

Blake spoke behind her. "Natalie had to leave?"

She turned to see Blake leaning against the wall in a handsome GQ pose. Man, she needed to get away from him. "Yes. And if you leave now, you can catch up to her."

"Why would I want to do that?"

His question took her by surprise. "You know. Saturday night. You could take her out. Eat dinner." *Make out behind the trees.*

He crossed the room and stopped a few inches from her. "I thought we already established she's not a good match for me."

Wow, he sure was something. Making it painfully obvious he was just fooling around with no intention of getting serious. She looked up at him and inched back. Her stupid schoolgirl crush was sucking the air out of the room. She stood still, hoping he couldn't hear her shallow breathing. "I just thought..."

"Do you have any thyme?"

She stared at him. "Time for what?"

He chuckled. "Not time. Thyme. When I was here earlier I noticed you have raw chicken in your fridge."

"You mean when you were snooping."

"Yep," he said unapologetically while he brushed past her. "I know a great chicken recipe."

Why was he headed toward her kitchen, instead of out the door? She wanted to tell him she had other plans, but she lacked the energy to argue with him. Plus, she hated to cook, and it looked like Blake was going to make dinner for her. "The spices are in the second cupboard. Help yourself."

"Found it." His voice was followed by the sounds of him searching for other kitchen items.

She should plop down on the couch and let him do it, but guilt forced her into the kitchen. "What else do you need?"

He listed off a few things, and she got them out. As he worked on the chicken, she pulled out a tube of crescent rolls and popped it open.

"Good idea. That will go great. I can make an easy green bean dish as well."

They worked alongside each other for a while in a companionable silence. The stifling awkwardness had dissipated, and Sidney was glad things were back to normal. She flipped on the radio and he rolled his eyes at her pop station but didn't say anything.

"You and your sister…looks like you don't get along?" He slid the glass casserole dish into the oven and raised an eyebrow at her.

What could she say to that? Natalie was just…Natalie. Self-absorbed. Never around when Sidney needed a sister, but always there when Natalie needed something from her. She sighed. "It's complicated."

Blake turned a chair around and sat backwards, his arms resting on the back of the chair. "How complicated?"

"She and I are very different." Sidney opened a cupboard, pulled out two plates and set them on the table.

"Thanks, Miss Obvious." He made a face.

"Don't you mean Captain Obvious?"

"I don't think I do. I think you might get a little bit of a seniority complex if I started attaching titles to you."

She huffed. "Well, at any rate," she said, setting down two forks. "Natalie's just too concerned about Natalie to notice anything else."

He sobered. "I could tell. She's very insecure."

Sidney squinted at him. Bold and brazen Natalie? The girl

willing to flirt with any breathing male within a sixty-mile radius? "You're kidding, right?"

He stared at her. "You don't see it?"

She sat down in the chair next to him. "I don't. She'll talk to any guy. She's been on more dates than anyone I know. She'd do anything to get a man's attention."

"But she doesn't get real with anyone, does she?"

Sidney laughed. "That's because there is no real with Natalie. She's surface. Fluff. She cares more about a broken nail than the economy or who the next president will be."

"Sad, isn't it?" Blake shifted in his chair.

"Pathetic."

"No, I mean, it's sad she doesn't have enough self-esteem to feel like she can offer up her opinion on things like the economy or the next president."

"She just doesn't care about that stuff." The smell coming from the oven made her mouth water.

"She cares. She's just too insecure to think anyone would want to know her opinion."

Sidney thought about Natalie. Was he right? Was she insecure? She hadn't always been so flighty and shallow. It had come upon her over time. "I don't know."

"Look at her. She wears tight clothes because she thinks her body is all she has to offer men. And I bet she hasn't had a significant relationship since high school."

Sidney hesitated. "You're right."

"She doesn't let anyone get close to her. The real her. She puts on a front, but inside she's hurting."

"How do you know all this?"

"I've taken some psych classes."

She grinned. "Like Shawn and Gus?"

His laughter filled the kitchen. "That's my favorite show on Netflix."

The timer buzzed and she hopped up to get the rolls. "I guess it's possible there's more to Natalie than meets the eye."

"There's more to most people."

Sidney eyed Blake as she set the rolls on the table. Why was he saying all this? He'd repeatedly told her he and Natalie wouldn't make a good match. What was his point? She didn't want to think about it, so she fiddled with the chicken, checking to see if the meat was done.

He came up behind her. "How does it look?"

The heat from the oven—and the heat coming from him standing so close behind her—made her uncomfortable. "Not done yet." She took a step, forcing him to move back.

He picked up the newspaper lying on her counter. "Do you have a pencil?"

She opened a drawer and handed him one. "You still do crossword puzzles?"

"You bet."

They worked on the puzzle for a while, until the timer for the chicken buzzed. She stood and crossed the room, grabbing the oven mitts, very aware that Blake was right behind her. She lifted the chicken out of the oven and Blake shut the door for her. Why did he have to smell so good? She set it on the hot plate, got out a serving spoon, and dished up the food.

Blake waited for her to sit. She picked up her fork and tentatively took a bite of the chicken. "This is good," she said.

"Thanks." He smiled, and she noticed how the laugh lines around his eyes were a nice feature on him. Made him look distinguished. Not old, really. Just gave him a more handsome look. Her cheeks burned when she realized she was staring at him, and she looked down to her lap.

"I've scheduled your first skydive for next weekend."

She coughed and almost choked on the food in her mouth. "You what?"

He pointed his fork at her. "No backing out."

"But…" She swallowed. "I don't know what I'm doing. Don't I need classes or something?"

Blake stabbed a green bean and grinned at her. "I've been an instructor for the last three years. It's no big deal."

Her face must have reflected her panic because he set his fork down and put his hand over hers. "They'll give you thirty minutes of instruction before we make the jump. And your first jump will be tandem, so there won't be any need to worry."

"What's tandem?"

"It's where we jump together. We wear harnesses, yours attached to mine. You'll be stuck to my chest. Don't worry, I've done it a hundred times."

Was she seriously going to jump out of an airplane with Blake? The thought of it both terrified and thrilled her. The terrified part wanted to back out of it, but the other part of her took over, and she nodded. "Okay."

He smiled. "You'll love it. I just know it."

After dinner they cleaned up the plates and then turned awkwardly to each other. Sidney motioned to the living room. "Well, I guess you'd better be going."

"You have Netflix, right? Do you want to watch Psych with me?"

The thought of him cozying up with her on the couch to watch TV jumped into her head and in a panic she blurted, "No! I've got to…" All thought left her head and she had no idea what excuse she could give him. She glanced down and saw her ring. "Call Ted. I've got to call him right now. He's expecting me."

She practically shoved Blake into the other room and toward the door. "So, see ya!"

He planted his feet on the floor and crossed his arms in a silent challenge. "Just a minute."

The only thing she could think of was getting him out of her apartment. "I'm really sorry. I need to call Ted right now. I kind of forgot about it and he'll be upset if I'm too late."

She sent him her most pleading expression, hoping he'd just go.

~

Blake observed Sidney's face and wondered what went wrong. He'd thought if he spent more time with her, got her to open up a little, she'd come clean about Ted. They'd had a good day together. He thought they'd made progress, but here she was, using Ted as an excuse to shove him out the door.

What had he done?

It wasn't the skydiving. He'd seen the curiosity in her eyes. She really did want to try it, even though it made her nervous. It wasn't that. She'd freaked out about the TV show. Why? It made no sense.

"Please, just go," she said, wringing her hands.

She really was distraught. He should leave. She must have been quite hurt in her past, to make her so afraid to let him get close to her. His heart ached for her, but what could he do about it? He turned and crossed the room toward the door. When he reached for the knob, he hesitated, and turned back to her. "Sidney…"

She looked up at him and he suddenly wanted to kiss her. He wasn't sure where that came from, but the thought of kissing her tempted him so much he almost leaned down to do it. Only, he couldn't.

She was still holding onto the lie. And kissing her would be forcing the issue. He would be telling her he knew, and he couldn't do that.

"What?" she said, searching his face.

If he couldn't kiss her, he'd at least leave her with the desire for it. He hooked her chin with his finger and tilted her head up, and leaned down until their lips were a breath apart. "Have a good night," he whispered.

And then he left.

CHAPTER 10

Sidney's heart thundered in her chest as she stared at the space Blake had occupied a moment before. Had he been about to kiss her? What was he doing flirting with *her* now? Of all the rotten things he could do, now he was shamelessly flirting with an almost married woman? She must look like an easy fling to him.

She gripped the back of the chair in an attempt to calm her shaking hands. Blake was completely wrong if he thought she would kiss him. She was an engaged woman. Well...sort of engaged. At least *he* thought she was, anyway. Who cared if it wasn't real? To Blake, she was taken. And now, he was playing games with her as well as Natalie?

But that wasn't the worst part.

She liked it. How could her body betray her like that? How could he make her pulse race? He was playing around with her heart, and it was going to end up broken. Again.

No, she couldn't let that happen. She had to stay away from him. Him and his flirty ways that didn't mean anything.

She had to kick him out of her life.

After a calming breath, she went into her bedroom and

put on her pajamas. It wasn't late, but she didn't want to do anything but crawl in bed and read. She arranged the pillows and sat back against them, book in hand. Just as she opened it, her phone made a pinging noise. Text message.

Phyllis: *Someone says you're engaged. I'm sure they're mistaken, as you would have told your mother if you were seriously dating anyone. Please call.*

Alarm shot through her. Who had told her mother? And what should she do about it? She had just swiped over to the phone app to call her mother when another text came in.

Chloe: *Sorry, I didn't know your mother wasn't aware of your engagement. Is it a secret? I think I spilled the beans. So sorry!*

How did Chloe find out? Must have been Blake. She hadn't thought about other people finding out when Mia suggested the idea. She dialed her mother.

"Sidney? Is it true?" Her mother's voice was strained.

For a split second, she thought about telling her mom the truth. How she was using the fake ring to get more clients, and how it was working. Business was actually picking up. Maybe her mom would be happy for her.

However, the image of her mother's disapproving frown popped into her head. She would look at her like she was disappointed. Like she should know better. She'd try to guilt her into telling the truth. And then Blake would find out she'd been lying.

"Sorry, we were waiting to tell everyone until we had a date set." The words came out before she fully processed them.

Her mother sucked in a breath. "She's getting married!" she yelled at someone in the room. A clamor of noise followed, and Sidney's heart sank.

"Mom, who's there?"

"Oh, I just called a few people over before texting you."

Panic gripped her. "Who?"

"Just a few of the neighbors. They're excited for you. Oh, and Natalie stopped by. She really wants to talk to you."

A muffled noise came through the line, before Natalie's voice hissed, "You're engaged to Blake? Why didn't you say anything? No wonder he moved back here. You could have told me, you made me look like an idiot!"

Oh no. How had this spiraled out of control? "I'm not engaged to Blake. I'm engaged to Ted."

"Wait!" her sister called out to the room. "It's not Blake she's engaged to, it's Ted!"

The voice changed back to her mother. "Who's Ted? And why did Blake move back here to be with you if you're marrying Ted?"

"No, Mom. You've got it all wrong. Blake has nothing to do with this."

"Well, when's the wedding? When can we meet him?"

Her father's voice came through from the background. "Phyllis, let me talk to her."

"Just a second, your father wants to say something."

More shuffling noises. "Pumpkin? Congratulations. We didn't even know you were dating anyone."

Sidney leaned back against the pillows and sighed. "Thanks, Dad."

"Your mother is dying to meet this young man. Can you invite him over for dinner tomorrow night?"

Sunday dinner? At her parents' house? Her throat tightened. "I don't know if he's free."

"Well, ask him. Call us back. I'll be in the doghouse if you don't."

Sidney believed him. Her mother wouldn't stop until she got what she wanted. Her stomach sank and she curled her legs under her. "Okay, Dad. Bye."

She hung up and tried to decide what would be better:

making up more lies about how Ted was out of town, or just calling and begging him to come to dinner.

Knowing her mother, the excuses would only hold her off for so long. She took in a deep breath and dialed up Ted.

"Hello?"

"Hey, it's Sidney, your fake fiancée." She nervously giggled and then felt ridiculous and clamped her mouth shut.

"Hey, what's up?"

"Listen, I've got a problem, and I was hoping you'd be able to help me out."

"Your computer acting up? I can come take a look at it Monday."

"No, that's not it." She stared down at her flannel pajamas. How was she supposed to ask him?

"What is it?" The concern in his voice made her feel twice as bad. Ted really was a nice guy.

"My parents found out about the fake engagement. They want to meet you."

"They what?" His voice cracked.

"I know it's a lot to ask, but business is going so well right now, I really don't want to give up the charade just yet. I promise I'll tell them we broke up in a few weeks. Would it be horrible for me to ask you to come to dinner tomorrow night and pretend we're engaged?"

She held her breath while he considered her request. "I guess I could do that."

Relief flooded over her. "Thank you! I promise this will be the only time."

She hung up then called her parents to tell them Ted would be joining them for Sunday dinner. After the conversation, she stretched out on the bed and stared up at her ceiling. She had either made a good decision, or a really, really bad one.

~

Ted came to pick her up at five o'clock. When she opened the door, he stood there in a white shirt and a tie, which she hadn't expected, but it looked good on his thin frame. Her mother would be pleased. It also went well with the cute top and white skirt she had chosen. "Hey," she said.

He nodded a greeting and held out his arm for her to take. "Who's all going to be at this dinner?"

Sidney walked with him to his car. "Just my parents. I think. Maybe Natalie."

He swallowed, and his Adam's apple bobbed. "Okay."

She turned to him. "I really appreciate you doing this. I know you didn't have to."

A grin formed on his face. "No problem. I've never been engaged before. Thought I'd try it out a little."

She giggled, then realized she sounded like she was flirting and stopped. "Thanks." She climbed into his car and he shut the door.

After he pulled out of the parking lot, he tapped the steering wheel and glanced at her. "I should probably ask how long your parents think we've been dating."

Sidney hadn't thought about it. "I don't know. Let's say, almost a year. Does that sound about right?"

He laughed and shrugged. "I have no clue. But it works for me." He pushed his glasses up his nose with his index finger. "When's the wedding?"

"We haven't picked a date yet. I think we'll keep saying that until we break it off."

"Okay."

Sidney fiddled with the strap on her purse. If they played it cool, everything would go well tonight. Just go in, eat the food, talk a little, and then leave. That's it. Easy, right? Her mother would be satisfied, and the world would keep on turning.

Sounded like a good plan to her.

"How did we meet?" Ted asked, tugging on his shirt collar.

"We met through Mia."

"Oh, right." Ted flipped on his turn signal.

"No need to be nervous. My parents are nice. Unless you count the time I snuck out in the middle of the night to T.P. a friend's tree. They weren't so nice then." She thought of how her parents had looked standing in the living room when she snuck back inside. She'd gotten a good lecture, and a weekend grounding.

Ted chuckled. "I can imagine."

"But, seriously, it should be easy."

He pulled up to her parents' home and cut the engine. He hopped out and walked around the car to open her door for her. She took his hand, in case anyone was watching.

Before they got to the door, her mother flew outside and assaulted her with a hug. She wore her purple Mumu, which she brought out for 'special' occasions. "So, this is Ted?" She turned and wrapped her arms around him. "Nice to meet you. Come on inside. I can't believe my daughter didn't even tell us she was dating anyone." She clicked her tongue in disapproval.

"Mom. Please. I didn't say anything because I didn't want you to embarrass me, like you're doing right now."

Her mother shook her head. "Nonsense. I'm Phyllis. Now come inside and meet everyone."

Everyone? Sidney's palms began to sweat and she inhaled, trying to remain calm. "Who?"

They stepped inside and her dad crushed poor Ted in a bear hug.

"This is Doug," her mother said, then pointed to the other

side of the room. "And this is our oldest daughter, Natalie, and our good family friend..."

She kept talking but the words sounded like mush as Sidney's gaze landed on the one person she hadn't expected to see.

Blake.

CHAPTER 11

The air whooshed out of Sidney's lungs and she felt lightheaded. What was Blake doing here? She blinked and looked around her childhood home, certain that he was a figment of her imagination. A ghost of a memory from growing up. Surely he'd be gone once she looked back.

Not so.

He shook hands with Ted, although the grimace on Blake's face was puzzling. Natalie looked like she'd won the blue ribbon at the county fair. "Blake was free tonight, so I invited him to come. Just like old times, right?" She looped her arm through his.

Sidney didn't want to be reminded about the last time they'd all shared a meal at her mother's table. In fact, she'd rather go lick the gutters clean than relive that evening.

"Why don't we all sit down? The rolls are ready to come out of the oven." Her mother clasped her hands together, her smile so wide Sidney wondered if it would pop off her face. At least she was happy.

They all went into the formal dining room and Ted pulled out a chair for Sidney. Blake sat directly across the table, and

Natalie quickly claimed the seat next to his. Her father sat at the head of the table while her mother flitted about setting the rolls out and making sure everyone had water. The table was already set, tablecloth and all. She'd even pulled out the cloth napkins.

"Phyllis, when you're ready, would you please say grace?" Her father bowed his head. Mom filled the last cup and then sat down and started the prayer.

The roast smelled delicious, and soon they were all passing around the food and the room filled with friendly chatter. Her mother turned to her. "I've been looking into wedding venues."

Her father frowned. Even though he'd greyed, he was still a formidable ex-military man. He'd gained a little weight since retirement, but not enough to hide his washboard stomach. "Phyllis, please. Let your daughter plan her own wedding."

Her mother wrung her hands. "But if we're going to have a spring wedding, we really need to book—"

Blake interrupted. "You have a date? To get married?" He stared at her pointedly. Whatever that meant.

"No," Sidney said. "We haven't set the date yet. We're still considering lots of options."

Ted put his arm around her. "We don't want to rush into anything."

She smiled up at him, grateful for his contribution. That was believable. But when she glanced at Blake his jaw was clenched and he looked upset about something. "Sure," he said under his breath.

Natalie cozied up to Blake. "When I get married, I'd love a winter wedding. Everything white." She looked at him. "What time of year do you want to get married?"

Sidney kicked her sister under the table, but Natalie just glared at her.

Blake cleared his throat. “I'd always thought a fall wedding would be nice, so that's what my wife and I had. Too bad it didn't stick.”

The room fell silent, everyone focusing on their plates. Sidney felt awful for Blake, and she mouthed, “I'm sorry,” to him.

He shrugged. “It's okay. People get divorced. It happens.”

Her father picked up the conversation. “Blake, how's your mother doing?”

And the awkwardness just kept coming. Nice. Sidney winced and tossed Blake another apologetic look.

“Not very well, I'm afraid.”

Her mother frowned. “I'm sorry to hear that. Is there anything we can do? I can take her a meal.”

Blake shook his head. “No, thank you. She's very independent. She'd be embarrassed.”

The conversation lulled and Sidney chewed her food. This was a fine evening full of uncomfortable situations. Maybe next they could all talk about how Asher cheated on her.

If she scarfed her food, perhaps she and Ted could leave soon. She stuffed a large piece of roast beef in her mouth. Everyone ate in silence for a few minutes.

Blake picked up his glass of water and took a sip. “How's Grayson? Is he still out in California?”

Her father puffed out his chest in pride. “Yes, he's working for NBC now. He's a writer for that show Forensic Science.”

“Great. He always wanted to work in Hollywood. Such a tough business, but I'm glad he's fulfilling his dreams.” Blake smiled and then turned to look at Sidney. “So, how did you and Ted meet?”

She swallowed the chunk of meat. “We met through Mia.”

He raised one eyebrow, and his grin seemed to hold a secret. "That's it?"

"Yes." She tried to keep the annoyance out of her voice, but wasn't too successful.

Blake leaned back in his chair, a smug smile now on his face. What was up with him? She wanted to smack him.

"Phyllis, you've outdone yourself," her father said. "This roast is divine." Everyone agreed, thanking her for cooking the meal.

Sidney noticed with relief that most people were almost done eating. Blake leaned forward and whispered, "Meet me under the table."

"What?" she whispered back.

He picked up his fork and dropped it on the floor. "Oops. Dropped my fork." He disappeared under the table.

Sidney pretended to drop her napkin and leaned down to retrieve it. "What are you doing?" she whispered.

"Reenacting a scene in our favorite movie." He winked at her, which caused her stomach to fill with butterflies.

"That's why you called me under here? To pretend you're Barbra Streisand?"

"No. I wanted to say you look uncomfortable, and to suggest we blow this joint."

"I can't! My parents want to get to know Ted!"

"Then leave Ted here." His smile seemed innocent, but he had a devilish gleam in his eyes.

"Very funny."

Natalie lifted the tablecloth and peeked under the table. "What are you guys doing?"

"Just testing a theory Sidney has."

Sidney tried to hold it in, but she couldn't and laughed. Natalie grunted in disgust and dropped the tablecloth back into place.

"She's no fun," Blake said, his face serious.

Sidney had nothing to say to that, and her back was starting to hurt, so she squirmed out from under the table. Blake sat up as well.

"Everything okay?" Her mother wore a disapproving glare on her face.

"Fine," Sidney said at the same time Blake said, "Yep." Ted seemed oblivious to anything going on.

Her mother's gaze darted between the two of them. "Since we are all done eating, maybe you can help me clear the table, Sidney."

Blake pointed a finger at her and mouthed the word, "Busted."

Sidney shot him a glare and stood, picking up her plate. "Sure, I'll help." She turned her back on Blake. Gathering up a stack of dirty dishes, she sighed. Almost done. Then she'd never have to go through this again.

Alone in the kitchen, she scraped the plates and started filling the dishwasher. Her mother came in and turned on the faucet. She looked at Sidney. "How long have you known Ted?"

"About as long as I've known Mia. Since college." This was true.

"And how long have you been dating?" She picked up the brush and scrubbed one of the plates.

"Almost a year." Not true. Guilt bubbled up in her chest. She hated lying to her mother.

Concern showed on her mother's face. "Your sister says you were out with Blake yesterday."

"Blake's a client. He hired me to find him a match. Plus, we're old friends. We were just catching up." All true, for the most part. She didn't have to mention how her crush had reared its ugly head, or how Blake had flirted with her.

Her mother nodded. "I understand. It's just, when you're in a relationship, it's important to put that person first." She glanced at Sidney. "And to be careful with other relationships."

Oh, heavens. Her mother thought she was going to cheat on her fake fiancé. "I know, Mom. It's not like that with Blake." At least, not in real life. Try telling that to her body when he was around.

Her mother smiled and put an arm around her. "Of course, dear. I just want what's best for you. That's all."

"I know."

"You and Blake have known each other a long time. You have a…special relationship."

Where was she going with this? Best to put away any thoughts of this nature. "Yes, but we're just friends." She hugged her mother, then left to gather more plates, glad that talk was over.

When the dishes were all in the dishwasher, Sidney wandered on into the living room where the rest of them were gathered around the computer. She rubbed the back of her neck. "Well, Ted, I've really got to get going to do that thing we discussed…so…" She pointed to the door.

Blake took a step toward her. "Ted's helping your dad with his computer. But since you've got somewhere to be, I'd be happy to give you a ride."

Ted waved his hand at her. "Sure. Blake can take you." He went back to clicking on the computer. That was Ted. Once he got involved with a computer, he didn't care about anything else. At least he loved his job.

She took the opportunity to flee. "Okay. Sounds good. See you later, Ted." Her mother frowned, but Sidney ignored it.

He mumbled his goodbye. They stepped outside into the cool evening air. "It's gotten chilly," she said, rubbing her arms, not really thinking it through.

Blake put his arm around her, pulling her close. "Here, I'll warm you."

Her silly crush went nuts, causing her heart to go into overdrive, tingles shooting across her skin. She wiggled out of his embrace. "Thanks, I'm fine." The last thing she needed was to react to his stupid flirting. She practically ran to his truck, her sandals slapping on the cement. She got into the passenger seat just as he reached her door.

He leaned on the truck. "You never let me open the car door for you." He frowned.

"Stop whining. I'm just faster than you are." She slapped his shoulder, expecting him to smile, but he didn't.

She tried to pull the door shut, but he held it open. "You let Ted."

She gaped at him. "You were watching out the window?"

"Your mom was a little anxious."

She laughed. "That's my mom for you." When he didn't respond, she sobered. "Why do you care, anyway?"

"I was always taught to open a door for a woman. It's a small thing, but it lets me show my respect. When you don't allow me to, it takes that away from me."

It didn't seem like a big deal to her, but since it meant something to Blake, she slipped out of the truck, shut the door and took a step back.

Blake stared at her for a few moments, and she met his gaze. His blue eyes assessed her, and then a hint of a smile touched his lips. He opened the door and then held out his hand to assist her into the truck. She took his hand, ignoring the wild zapping of electricity, and stepped up into the seat.

He allowed a full smile, and shut her door. Neither one said anything as he drove her home. When he stopped in front of her house, she sat there and let him come around to open the door. He again held out his hand to help her out of the truck.

After she stepped out on the cement, he didn't release her hand but held it as he walked her to her door. It didn't seem flirty. It felt deeper, more like they had a connection—and she didn't want to break it. She turned to look at him, and he captured her other hand as well. "Thank you," he said, his voice low.

All of a sudden, the whole door thing didn't seem so silly anymore. It seemed important somehow, although she couldn't fully understand. She blushed, and she hoped he couldn't see her pink cheeks in the moonlight. "You're welcome."

He held her hands for a few seconds longer before releasing them and stuffing his own in his pockets. He looked like he wanted to say something, but kept silent.

"Thanks for bringing me home," she said, mostly to fill the silence.

"Yeah." He blinked and ran a hand through his hair. "Anytime." He took a step back. "Good night, Sidney."

He turned and walked down the sidewalk toward his truck. "Good night," she said, her voice a whisper.

CHAPTER 12

Blake spent the next week trying to get Sidney off his mind, which was fairly easy to do while he was at work. Treating his patients was a decent distraction. But as soon as he came home to an empty house, fixed a meal by himself, and sat alone, he couldn't think of anything else. Not even finishing up the kitchen renovation took his mind off her.

Sidney had actually brought Ted to meet her family. This lie of hers was taking on a life of its own. It was almost becoming an obsession for him to figure her out. Why was she going to such great lengths? It couldn't only be about the business. There had to be more to it.

On Thursday, Sidney left him a message saying she found him another match. Funny thing was, he couldn't care less about being matched anymore. He'd much rather spend his free time with Sidney. He told himself it was because her lie was driving him nuts and he just wanted her to tell him the truth, but he knew there was more to it than that. Spending time with Sidney was fun.

He didn't return her call. Instead, on Friday evening, he

ran to the store and bought her favorite board game, and showed up on her doorstep. He rang the bell and waited for her to answer.

Sidney cracked the door. "Blake? What are you doing here?" She sounded tired.

"I want a re-match."

"A what?" She pulled the door open further and he glanced at her comfortable T-shirt and sweat pants. For some reason, knowing she was home alone on a Friday night made him happy.

He lifted the Monopoly game. "Last time you beat me, rather unfairly I'd say. I think I deserve a do-over."

She curled a strand of her brown hair behind her ear, a smile playing on her lips. "It was fair and square, and you know it. Besides, you usually were the one who won. I deserved one small victory."

"One? I seem to remember it differently, Miss Queen of the Railroads."

She grinned, but when their eyes met, she sobered. "Sorry, I can't tonight."

"Why not?"

She sighed. "Because it isn't a good idea, me being engaged and all."

There it was. That wall she'd been putting up in the name of Ted. He had to make her see she could trust him. "Sidney, we're just friends. I swear I'm not here to break up you and Ted."

Indecision played across her features, but in the end, she shook her head. "I really can't." She started closing the door and he panicked.

"Wait. You can start with $500 extra." That got her attention, and she stopped, so he sweetened the pot. "And I'll give you B&O Railroad."

She paused, thinking it over. "Throw in Boardwalk and you've got a deal."

"What? No way. I'd be signing my death certificate."

She smirked. "Don't like a challenge? Okay then, if you'd rather go home..."

"You are evil," he said, holding in a chuckle. "Okay, fine, you get to start with Boardwalk and B&O, and when you still lose, you have to do the chicken dance outside." He pushed his way into her apartment and set the game on the coffee table.

She shut the door. "Fine by me. But if you lose, you have to ding-dong ditch the haunted mansion."

"Deal." He sat down on the couch and opened the box. Sidney sat on the opposite side and started setting up the banker's tray.

"I want to be the shoe."

"Like you've ever been anything else." He tossed her the die cast game piece.

"Sometimes I like to be the iron, so I can iron the board." She grinned at him, and he laughed. He liked this Sidney. The laid back one. The one who wasn't holding him at arm's length and putting up Ted walls.

They set up the game and started rolling the dice. Sidney grabbed up several properties right away, while he landed on chance and had to pay a fine. As they played, Blake wondered what he could do to make this Sidney stay around a while.

At one point, Sidney left the room to use the restroom, and Blake picked up her phone. As a prank, he loaded his favorite classic rock songs in her playlist, then he placed her phone back on the table. He smiled to himself when she came back.

The game quickly turned into a game of "Let's give Sidney money," as he continued to land on her properties. He picked up the dice. "Six or ten, six or ten," he said under his breath.

"There's no escape. Mama needs a new hotel."

The smile on Sidney's face was worth his pretend financial devastation. He tossed the dice and rolled a seven. "Aw, man."

"Ha!" She grabbed her card and read it. "You owe me $750."

He looked at his dwindling pile of cash. "Would you take a kiss instead?" He hadn't meant to say it, the words just slipped out. Instead of apologizing, like he should have done, he raised his eyes to meet hers in a silent challenge. He was intensely curious what she would say.

Her look of shock melted into something he couldn't quite read. She stared at him, and then raised one eyebrow. "I don't think Ted would like that, do you?"

He felt the progress he'd made slip away as she folded her arms across her chest. She was shutting him out again. "I was kidding," he said in a lame attempt to make it all better.

"Yeah? Well, you're going to have to mortgage something if you don't have the cash, buck-o. Unless you want to do my dishes for me."

"You'd let me out of my fine if I wash your dishes?"

She rubbed her hands together in a greedy way. "You bet."

"Done." He stood and crossed the room. Sidney followed him into the kitchen. When he saw the counter and sink full of dirty dishes, his jaw hit the floor. "What did you do in here?"

Her laughter bounced off the walls. "I volunteered to take a couple of meals to some women at Mom's church. I was going to start cleaning up when you rang the doorbell."

"You played me!" Before he thought about it, he grabbed her and started tickling her sides like he used to when they were kids.

She squirmed and tried to shout while laughing. "Don't!" The word barely came out through her giggles. "Stop!"

"Don't stop? Okay." He continued to tickle as she fought against him.

Her fists pounded on his shoulder as she wriggled to get away. He stopped his assault and let her settle down. "You going to admit you played me?" he said in her ear, his heart hammering in his chest while he held her tight.

"Yes," she said, breathless. She looked up at him and he got lost in the depths of her brown eyes. He was surprised at how nice it felt to have her in his arms. Her lips were inches from his, and he couldn't stop himself from gazing at them.

Before doing something that would surely make her walls go up, he let her go and turned to the sink. "Guess I'd better get started."

Sidney opened the dishwasher. "If you scrape the food and rinse them, I'll stack them in the dishwasher."

He nodded and picked up a mixing bowl, his pulse still racing. The room was charged with so much electricity, the hairs on the back of his neck stood up. Did Sidney feel it, too?

As they worked together, she relaxed, and the mood turned light again. "How's your Mom?" she asked.

"She's doing better."

"That's good. She's lucky to have you near."

Blake smiled. "You ready to go skydiving tomorrow?"

She whacked him on the arm. "You're such a dork for making me jump out of a plane. I'm scared out of my gourd."

"What does that even mean? When were you ever in your gourd?"

She rolled her eyes. "Funny. What if the parachute doesn't open?"

"Don't worry. There's a back-up. Plus, they hardly ever

fail. Statistically, it's safer to skydive than it is to drive across town." He handed her a pot.

"I'll take your word for it. If I die, though, you're in big trouble."

"Since we'll be jumping tandem, if you die I'm going with you."

She squinted at him. "I'm not sure if that makes me feel better or not."

He picked up a wooden spoon covered in spaghetti sauce. "It should. I'm not ready to die." After rinsing the spoon, he handed it to her, looking into her eyes. "When I die, I want no regrets." Wow, he was being bold, wasn't he? He'd better tone it down a notch, or she'd put up another Ted wall.

A sad look flitted across her face, and she bent over to place the spoon in the dishwasher. "My only regret is Asher."

She said it so softly, he didn't know if she meant it for his ears or not. But it was the first sign that she was ready to talk about it, so he jumped on it. "What happened?"

She took in a deep breath and let it out slowly. "The short version is he cheated on me."

He waited for her to continue, and when she didn't, he asked, "And what's the long version?"

She stared down the pan she was holding. "We dated for more than a year. I thought things were getting serious between us. He kept talking about marriage and settling down. He had all these high aspirations. Wanted to be a senator after climbing the political ladder."

Her pain was evident on her face, and she swallowed a few times before continuing. "He took me out to eat for Valentine's Day. I thought he was going to propose." She looked up at him. "I suppose he might have if things hadn't gone the way they did."

Blake was so afraid of pushing her, he said nothing while

he scrubbed a casserole dish. She'd continue when she was ready.

"Asher went to the bathroom and left his cell on the table. He never did that. He was so protective of that thing. I figured he had important business he was always conducting. When a text message came through, I picked it up. Imagine my surprise when I found the message was from another woman, asking if they were still meeting later that evening."

"Awful."

"It gets worse. I scrolled up to see more of the conversation, to see if it was a business meeting. The texts were...well, let's just say it was obvious they were having an affair. And when he talked about me, he called me...The Stiff." She blinked and squared her shoulders like she didn't want to waste one more tear on him. "Apparently *Patty* wasn't the right kind of woman to be on his arm, but she was the one he wanted in his bed."

Blake fought the urge to pull her into his arms. It wouldn't be a good thing. She was opening up to him, and he couldn't push it. But he knew just how she felt, after being treated almost the same way by Melody. His throat constricted. "I'm so sorry," he said, his voice husky.

She held her hand out for the casserole dish. "When he came back to the table and found out I knew about Patty, he tried to convince me I'd misunderstood, that I had read it wrong. He had an explanation for everything." Her voice lowered to almost a whisper. "His lies were so convincing, I almost believed him."

"You wanted to believe him." He unstopped the sink and wiped his hands on a towel.

Sidney nodded and closed the dishwasher. "I didn't want to be the stiff." A single tear traced down her cheek.

He took a step to close the distance between them, not

wanting to scare her off but needing to comfort her. He slowly raised his hand and wiped the tear with his thumb.

Sidney closed her eyes, another tear escaping. He put his hands on her waist and gently pulled her to him. She laid her head on his chest and melted into him. He put his arms around her and simply held her close, breathing in her scent while his heart went into overdrive. He cradled her until her tears stopped and she pulled back.

"Sorry, I don't know what's gotten into me."

"No need to apologize." Before she had the chance to lie and put up another Ted wall, he let go of her and walked into the living room, even though he would have rather stayed there holding her. "I guess I have to concede. You own too much property for me to win."

She opened her mouth wide. "You're…giving up? You?"

He shrugged and stuck his fists into his pockets. "I know when I'm defeated."

"Well, I guess there's only one thing to do." An evil little smile formed on her lips, but he couldn't figure out why.

"What?"

"We've got to go to the haunted mansion."

~

Sidney giggled as she crouched down behind the large bush. Blake was on all fours, peeking around the foliage. "I can't believe you're making me do this."

"A bet is a bet, buck-o. You gotta pay up."

He sneezed. "Man, what kind of bush is this? It's making my nose itch."

"Just go ring the bell."

He glared at her, which didn't work very well because he couldn't hide his smile. "Easy for you to say. Did you look at those steps? They're all rotted out. I think I'm going to fall in if I try to run up them."

"Step lightly." She pushed his shoulder. "Get to it, I'm getting a cramp."

"We're not crawling through poison oak, are we?"

"No, and quit stalling."

"Okay, okay." He jumped to his feet and ran up the cracked cement walkway. She giggled as he ran up the steps, trying to avoid the decaying wood. He pushed the doorbell and ran back down.

The porch light lit up and Sidney squealed. She sprang to her feet and joined Blake in his mad dash to get away. Her heart pounded from the adrenalin as they ran across the yard. Blake pulled ahead of her and she grabbed onto his shirt to keep from being left behind.

He tripped, and a loud ripping noise rang out as he struggled to catch himself before hitting the ground. Sidney giggled as he slowed to look at his ripped shirt.

"What are you kids doing?" an old man yelled from the doorway. "Get off my lawn!"

They both burst out laughing and then sprinted the rest of the way to the sidewalk. They slowed as they neared Blake's truck. "You tore my shirt!" Blake said as he opened the passenger door.

"Technically you tore it. I was just holding it." She climbed into the seat, breathless from the running.

He leaned into the cab. "You think so, huh?" A playful smile tugged at his lips.

He was so close she could smell his aftershave, and her heart did that crazy crush thing again. She shoved him away. "Yes, your fault. Now get in and drive."

He chuckled and obliged.

CHAPTER 13

Sidney sat on the cold metal folding chair in the small classroom. Blake sat beside her, an encouraging smile on his face. The skydiving instructor, a balding man in his late thirties, was energetically telling her what she was about to experience.

A few other people sat in there with them, and most of them looked excited. Sidney glanced at a sign on the wall that read, 'If at first you don't succeed, skydiving is not for you.' She thought she might throw up. Blake reached over and squeezed her hand.

When it came time to put on the gear, she thought she would lose it. "Why did you talk me into this?"

"Because you're going to love it." He helped her slip the harness around her middle. When his fingers brushed her skin, the tingles took over, making her entire body buzz. Maybe being strapped to Blake wouldn't be so bad. He handed her a pair of goggles and a helmet.

"What makes you so sure?"

He clasped her shoulders in his strong hands and looked into her eyes. She knew she shouldn't meet his gaze. His eyes held some crazy magical power over her, and her knees melted when she looked at them. But she had no choice, and she silently cursed her weakness as she looked into his cool blue eyes.

"Remember when we would go to the park as kids? You would always run off to find the tallest tree to climb. I once asked you why you did that. You told me it was the closest you'd get to flying with the birds."

He remembered that? Why did he care so much about her wish to fly when he was sneaking off and making out with Natalie? Blake was a mystery. A frustrating but very handsome mystery. She swallowed. "I was seven."

"But you spoke from your heart." He clicked the metal ring into place and turned her around. "Now, we're going to board the plane. When it's time to jump, I'll hitch us together."

Her heart leapt into her throat. She really was going to do this. With Blake. Was she insane? She'd given up doing insane things long ago. Being cautious was better. You don't get hurt when you think things through.

As they walked out to the small plane, Sidney shook her hands, trying to get rid of the nerves. Blake said he'd done this a million times. She'd be fine. If she hated it, all she had to do was close her eyes and pretend she was on some scary amusement park ride. At least she loved those. Hmm. Maybe Blake was right. Maybe she would like this.

They got to the steps and Blake climbed into the plane, then extended his hand. She stared at it. "Do you trust me?" he asked.

"Yes," she said without hesitation, which made her blink in surprise. She did trust him. Last night she'd trusted him enough to tell him things she hadn't even told Mia. She'd thought she couldn't bear to reveal Asher's hurtful name for her to anyone, but she'd told Blake.

The realization startled her and she took a step back. Why had she told Blake, anyway? Because they were friends? Or was it because she wanted something more? What was it about Blake that made her say and do things she never would with anyone else? She couldn't afford to make more out of this than there was. Her heart couldn't take another shatter from Blake. Sure, he was flirting, but she knew he wasn't serious about her.

"Take my hand."

His command brought her out of her thoughts and she grabbed his hand. She was being stupid. He'd said they were friends, and friends told each other stuff. That's all. She didn't need to read anything into the situation. That was what had gotten her into trouble last time.

Blake pulled her close. "You okay?" he whispered in her ear.

"Fine." She plastered on a smile.

"Good. Because the fun is about to begin." He motioned to a seat. "You'll need to be strapped in for take-off."

She sat down and pulled the seatbelt tight after clicking it in. The instructor closed the door and they waited while someone did some final flight checks. Her pulse thrummed as she gripped her seat and the engine started.

Blake leaned over. "Remember the rope over the lake?" He practically had to scream over the noise.

"Yeah."

"It's another reason I think you'll love this."

She did remember the summer they tied a rope to a branch that hung over the lake. They'd run and swing out as far as they could, then let go and see how big of a splash they could make. She smirked. "I remember you got a tick. Right on your back side."

He cringed. "That was an unfortunate incident."

"My mom had to pull it off." She nudged him and they both laughed.

"Well, how was I supposed to reach it?" His face turned red, and she laughed again.

The plane began moving, and Sidney swallowed her nerves. This was it. They were going up. The only way down was to jump.

The plane waited for a minute, then accelerated forward and took off. Sidney grabbed Blake's hand as they climbed higher. Soon they were circling, and the instructor opened the door.

The other jumpers went first. Some of them went solo, while two went tandem like she and Blake. When it was their turn, she stood and Blake ushered her closer to the door. There were several metal clinking sounds as Blake clipped himself to the back of her harness. He tugged on them to make sure they were secure. "Are you ready?" he shouted.

She shook her head. "No."

He put his arms around her, pulling her back to his chest. "Don't worry," he said in her ear. "I've got you." The deep intonation of his voice combined with his close proximity made her heart do funny things in her chest. "Now, cross your arms and hold onto the shoulder straps."

She did as he said, her knuckles white from clenching so hard. She could do this. She could jump from a plane.

"Lift your legs up to your chest."

When she lifted up, she felt like she was in a baby carrier, hooked onto Blake's chest. He stepped to the open door. "On the count of three."

She nodded.

"One. Two." He hesitated, and she thought she was going to pass out from the anxiety. "Three."

She closed her eyes as he jumped. The wind whistled past her at an alarming rate, like she'd stuck her head out of the car on the interstate. It pushed against her cheeks, distorting her face. Her stomach dropped and she screamed, but as soon as they were away from the plane, a peaceful silence settled in and she opened her eyes.

She'd seen photographs taken from above, but the view before her was more breathtaking than she'd anticipated. And the feeling of rushing through the air, flying…it was incredible. Exhilarating. Her pulse raced and her senses felt heightened. She stretched her arms out. Speaking was almost impossible with the wind, so she just let out a happy whoop.

From this vantage point, she could see the curvature of the earth. The farm fields in patches of greens and browns. The clouds. It was amazing.

Blake shifted and they started spinning, like a snowflake in the wind. She screamed, enjoying the dizzying effect it had on her brain. He stopped the spinning and let her enjoy the free fall for a few moments longer, but it felt almost like an eternity. Time seemed to work differently as they fell at a dizzying speed toward the earth.

Blake reached up and pulled the cord. They jerked when the parachute deployed and caught their rapid fall. The air no longer rushed past her but turned into a brisk breeze instead.

"What did you think?" he asked.

"That was awesome!" she shouted.

He laughed. "I knew you'd love it."

"I don't know why I was so scared."

Blake pointed. "There's the lake."

She looked out over the town, the miniature buildings and the tiny cars. The gentle descent combined with the close proximity to Blake made her stomach do flips. She tried to ignore the way her skin came alive when they touched. They took turns pointing out landmarks while

Blake steered them so they would land in the field near the airport.

As they neared the ground, she found herself disappointed. That had been the most amazing thing she'd ever done...and it was over. She lifted her feet as instructed. Their descent was slow enough that Blake landed on his feet. Blake unhooked them and Sidney turned around, unable to hide the excitement rushing through her. "That. Was. Amazing!"

She took off her helmet and goggles, tossing them on the grass. "I can't believe the feeling of flying through the air. It was unlike anything I've ever experienced."

Blake grinned, peeling off his goggles as well. "I'm glad I made you do it."

Before she thought much about it, she threw her arms around his neck and hugged him. He seemed stunned at first, but he snapped out of it and pulled her close to him. Her heart pounded loudly in her ears. As the tingles coursed through her body, she knew she'd made a mistake and tried to push back, but his hold on her was too strong. She looked up at him, and he stared at her, all playfulness gone. He was gazing at her, and it made her stomach feel like she'd jumped from the plane again.

She couldn't look him in the eyes, so her gaze landed on his lips, which was dumb, but all thought left her brain. His lips moved closer, and she felt a force stronger than any magnet pulling her to him.

Their lips met and her senses exploded. His kiss was tentative. Gentle. But the feelings it stirred up were strong. She kissed him back, before her brain could register what they were doing. She didn't want to think. All she wanted was for this moment to last forever.

Being in his embrace, his lips moving over hers, felt like the world had stopped and nothing else mattered. She grew dizzy as he kissed her more passionately.

And then, like an unwanted guest at a party, her sister's voice came into her head. *Do you remember when you kissed me behind the trees in our backyard?*

Snapping out of her Blake-induced coma, she shoved herself away from him. What was she doing? She couldn't kiss Blake!

She turned to flee, but he grabbed her arm. "Sidney… wait."

She turned back to him. "I'm engaged, Blake. What do you think you're doing?"

He winced. "I'm sorry. I didn't mean to."

His words sent a stabbing pain through her chest. She wanted to get away from him. Run from the feelings he created in her. Run from the way he had carelessly kissed her, like it was no big deal to him. He must have read her thoughts, because he pulled her to him and wrapped his arms around her, forcing her to stay. "Please forgive me. It was a mistake, I promise."

The look on his face stopped her cold. He looked pained. He regretted kissing her. Nice. This was worse than his flirting! She wanted to sink into a hole in the ground.

He pulled back, his face pleading. "I'm sorry. Can we just forget it happened?"

What was she supposed to say to that? If she said no and stomped off, she'd look like a stupid child. Especially when she'd been sucked into the kiss as well and had kissed him back. She was probably at fault as much as he was. She took in a deep breath and let it out slowly. "Fine."

He let go of her and began gathering up his parachute. "I don't know what got into me. The excitement of the jump, I guess."

She picked up her helmet and goggles and mumbled, "I guess." If he was trying to make things better, he wasn't doing it right. She felt dead inside.

"I'm glad you liked the jump. Maybe we can go again in a few weeks."

Not likely. She swallowed back the words and instead forced a smile. "Sure."

They didn't speak as they took off their gear and gathered their things. When they got to his truck, she waited for him to open her door, even though she wanted to hop in to annoy him.

He opened the door and she climbed in. "Do you want to go grab some dinner?"

I'd rather eat glass. She coughed into her fist. "Sorry, I have to go into the office tonight and get caught up on some things."

He shut her door and climbed into the driver's seat. "I could help."

A knot formed in the pit of her stomach. How was she going to get out of this? She'd just told him she'd forget about the kiss and pretend it never happened. "It's just data entry, and boring stuff. I'm sure you don't want to—"

"I don't mind. It will give me something to do."

Sidney bit the inside of her cheek. If she protested too much, he'd think she was mad at him. Or worse, being a baby about the kiss. She sighed. "Okay."

"We can order Chinese. Your favorite still the cashew chicken?"

"Sounds delicious." Super. She was stuck spending the evening with Blake.

CHAPTER 14

Blake held the take out and the drinks, and still managed to open the door to Blissfully Matched without dropping anything. Sidney looked up from her computer and rushed around her desk.

She took the paper sack and set it down on her desk. “Sorry, I probably should have gone with you to get dinner.” She frowned.

It hadn’t bothered him. In all honesty, he was glad she wasn’t shoving him out the door. He’d royally messed up by kissing her. He hadn’t meant to do it. His body had just taken over, and he’d found he couldn’t control the urge anymore. Stupid. She’d put up her Ted wall so fast his head spun.

“No problem.” He pulled the chair closer to his side of her desk.

Sidney lifted the containers out of the sack, handing over his broccoli beef and a fork and doing her best not to look at him. The aromas filled the small space, and his stomach growled. She sat down and started on her meal.

The tension in the room was stifling. Why had he insisted

on spending time with her this evening? She didn't want him around. He was probably hurting the situation more than helping it. But something in him wouldn't let go.

Kissing Sidney had been amazing. She'd ignited a fire in him years ago, and kissing her again had rekindled the flame. Kissing Melody had never been that way. There was something between him and Sidney he couldn't deny.

Sidney looked up from her take out. "What are you doing next Friday night?"

He froze. She was asking him out? Maybe he was misreading her. Maybe she wasn't upset about the kiss. "Nothing."

"Great. Your next match will meet you at Thai Land, on Fifth Street. Wear something nice."

He should have seen that one coming. Forcing a smile, he stabbed a piece of broccoli with his fork. "Okay. What's her name?"

"Angie Nicholson. And don't be so picky this time."

He wrinkled his nose. "Is this how you talk to your clients?" She opened her mouth to respond, but he continued, cutting her off. "I see how you do it, now. You intimidate your clients so they feel obligated to say they found a match."

She rolled her eyes. "Oh, puh-leeze. Stop being such a baby about it. Admit you were a little picky with Chloe."

"I admit nothing."

"Fine. Be like that. But Angie is a dear, and you need to give her a chance."

"Of course." He faked enthusiasm. The only girl who interested him right now was sitting across from him. The thought startled him and he swallowed. Sidney was doing everything she could to push him away. What kind of crazy notion did he have that she might get over it and become interested in him? Why was he doing this to himself?

She smiled. "Good. Meet Angie at six. Be nice."

"I'm always nice."

She picked up her soda and took a sip. "Mm hmm."

"Are you implying something?"

"What about all those times you and Grayson would sit on me until I did what you wanted? How nice was that?"

Blake let out a hearty laugh. "I'd forgotten about that."

"You weren't the one scarred for life."

He took another bite of his meal, assessing her. She was beginning to relax again, and joke around with him. How could he keep her this way? After he swallowed, he said, "You're being a little dramatic."

"Maybe so. But you have to admit, you and Grayson did your share of torturing me."

He chuckled. "You dished it right back, if I recall. I remember a bucket of water landing on my head when I entered the kitchen."

"Payback for the whoopee cushion." She grinned and then sobered. "Do you and Grayson keep in touch?"

"We've chatted a few times online, but not much."

"Yeah." She stared at her food. "Me, too."

The saddened look in her eyes made his gut clench. "You're not close anymore?"

She shrugged. "He's focused on his career right now. Rarely comes back to see us. The last time he visited was Christmas—three years ago."

Silence stretched as she played with her food a little while longer. He wanted to take her hand but knew that was a bad idea. "I'm sorry."

"It's okay. I know he's busy. I just…" She let her voice trail off.

"You miss him."

She nodded. "I watch Forensic Science each week, even

though it's a bit too bloody for me, just because I know he's a part of it."

"That's really sweet."

His cell phone rang out Bohemian Rhapsody, and he caught Sidney's 'oh brother' look. He smiled as he swiped the front and answered. "Hey, Ma. What's up?"

A muffled sound came through the line, and then she whispered, "Blake."

His throat tightened. "Mom? You okay?"

Silence.

He stood, his heart racing. "Mom?"

The line went dead and he cursed.

Sidney jumped out of her chair. "What's wrong?"

"I don't know." He dialed her number again as he headed to the door. "She was fine this morning. I've got to go check on her."

"I'm coming with you." She grabbed her purse.

After Sidney locked the door, they ran to his truck. His mother's phone went directly to voice mail. He tossed his cell to Sidney. "Keep trying." He put the truck in gear and tore out of the parking lot.

Sidney's hands shook as she fiddled with the phone. "What did she say?"

"Just my name. She could barely speak."

"Dear heavens." Her face drained of color and her eyes grew wide.

He wanted to say something to reassure her, but no comforting words came. The red lights seemed to take an extra-long time, and he tapped the steering wheel. Maybe he should call 911. But what if it wasn't an emergency? His mother would be livid.

When they got to her house, he stopped in the driveway and both of them ran to the front door. He tried the handle, but it was locked. "Mom?" he called, lifting the plant to get the key hidden under the pot.

No one answered, and he unlocked the door and ran inside. His mother lay on the floor in the kitchen, her phone in her hand. Blood pooled on the tile under her head, which sported a large gash. A chair lay on its side. He gently shifted her so he could look at the wound.

"There's a first aid kit under the sink." He looked up at Sidney and she nodded. She opened the cupboard and brought it to him.

He pressed some gauze to the injury to stop the bleeding. His mother stirred and he breathed a sigh of relief. "Mom, what happened?"

Her eyelids fluttered open. "Blake. I knew you'd come."

"Are you okay? What were you doing, Ma?"

She pointed up. "The light was flickering again."

He groaned inwardly. "I told you I would fix it." But he hadn't. He'd let it go. Guilt swarmed in on him like angry bees.

"I know." She winced when he lifted the gauze to look. "I shouldn't have messed with it."

"The fall didn't knock you out, because you had time to call me."

She raised her hand and took hold of the gauze, pressing it to her head. "I think I fainted when I saw the blood."

Sidney crouched down beside her. "You scared us, Mrs. Wellington."

His mother's gaze fell on Sidney for the first time. She looked at Blake, then back at Sidney. She struggled to sit up. He placed his hand on her back and steadied her. "I'm sorry. Did I interrupt something?"

"I was just eating dinner with an old friend. You remember Sidney Reed?"

His mother smiled. "Of course. Sidney, you've sure grown up."

Suddenly, she burst out laughing. "That's what I keep hearing."

~

Sidney exhaled relief as Blake drove her home. She'd been so afraid something serious had happened. Thank goodness it was just a fall, with nothing broken. Blake had examined his mother's injury and proclaimed it minor. Gave them a good scare, but she'd be fine.

Blake scowled and hit the steering wheel. "I should have fixed that light for her."

"You couldn't have known she'd get up on a chair and mess with it."

He pulled into her parking lot and cut the engine. "She asked me to look at it days ago."

Sidney felt his pain. "So, you're human."

"I knew the flickering bugged her. It wouldn't have taken me long to look at it." He ran his hand through his hair.

"You fixed it tonight."

He gave her a flat look. "A little too late, don't you think?"

She placed a comforting hand on his shoulder. "It's not your fault."

"I could have gone over there. I've just been too preoccupied with—" He stopped and clenched his fist on the steering wheel.

"With what?"

"My own stupidity," he said, under his breath as he got out. He opened her door for her.

He walked her to her door, his shoulders slumping. "Don't be so hard on yourself."

"It could have been so much worse."

"But it wasn't. She's fine." Sidney didn't know what else to say to make him feel better. She pulled him into a hug and laid her head on his chest. "You're a good man, Blake."

He patted her back but didn't say anything. After he left, she plopped down on her couch, trying to ignore the empty feeling in her chest.

CHAPTER 15

Sidney looked at the clock. Six-thirty. Blake had been on his date with Angie for a half-hour now. She went back to her book, staring at the same page she'd been on for the past ten minutes. None of the words sank in. As soon as she started reading, visions of Blake and Angie filled her head and she couldn't concentrate. Frustrated, she tossed the book on the coffee table and stood. Time to do something else.

She opened the closet and took out her running shoes. It had been a while since she'd put them on, but her restlessness wouldn't leave. Running would be the perfect thing. She quickly changed and pulled her hair into a ponytail.

She strapped her phone to her arm and plugged in her earphones. When she pressed the button to play her favorite music, instead of One Direction, she heard the opening guitar riff from *Stairway to Heaven*.

What? She scrolled through and saw that Blake had managed to put a bunch of his songs on her playlist.

Ugh. She swiped until she found her own playlist and

turned up her favorite pop song, letting the music flow into her soul.

When she stepped outside, she took a deep breath. The late evening sun cast long shadows, and the cool breeze felt refreshing. She started jogging on the sidewalk, down a residential street.

Blake hadn't contacted her all week. She wasn't sure what she was expecting, but for some reason his lack of communication was driving her nuts. She'd gotten used to seeing him pop up for one reason or another, but now, his absence left a hole.

Maybe he'll come over after his date, like last time.

She shook her head to clear the thought away. No. She didn't need to see Blake. He needed to leave her alone so she could get over her stupid crush and get on with her life.

She turned down Ash Avenue, picking up her pace. It was dangerous keeping Blake as a friend. The kiss proved that. He was just messing around, and she…what was she doing, falling in love?

Oh heavens. That couldn't be right. She couldn't fall in love with Blake. Not again. She ran faster, feeling the burn in her lungs and an ache in her muscles.

Last time, she was sixteen years old. Everything had been so dramatic at that age. Her massive crush. Her first kiss. Her humiliation when Blake called her a little girl. It had caused such heartache, she had learned to push her crazy impulses away and rely on her level head.

And now her head was telling her to stay away from flirty men who just wanted nothing more than a fun time. She huffed in disgust.

Her phone pinged, letting her know a text had come through. She pulled it out of her arm band and looked at the message.

Phyllis: *Can you come over?*

Sidney looked up at the street sign. She actually wasn't too far away from her parents' house. She jogged in place while she texted back.

Sidney: *I can be there in ten minutes.*

Phyllis: *Thank you. See you soon!*

When she reached her parents' street, she had a nice sweat going. Her lungs begged for a break and she slowed to a walk to cool down. She pulled her earphones out as she came up the walkway.

Her mother had the door open before she reached the steps. "Come on in." She wore an overly wide smile on her face.

Sidney's Spidey senses kicked in, and she glanced around. "What's going on, Mom?"

Her mother took her hand and led her into the living room. The first thing she noticed was Ted sitting on the couch, his hands on his knees. Then she saw her father, looking uncomfortable sitting in a folding chair someone had brought in. Then her gaze landed on Reverend Joseph.

Oh crud.

She sucked in a breath and looked to her mother.

"Sidney, I thought we could all sit down and have a conversation."

Panic enveloped her as she looked down at her shirt, stuck to her skin by the large sweat stain on her front. Nice. Her underwear was also creeping where it shouldn't be, but now wasn't the time to fix it. "Mom, I was just out running…"

Reverend Joseph stood and extended his hand. He was the kind of guy you'd see on television playing a reverend. Young, but not too young. Mildly good-looking. A wide smile you could trust. "Nice to see you again, Sidney. Your mother tells me you're getting married?"

Her throat closed up and she had difficulty breathing. Was

it too much to hope for a zombie apocalypse to start up right about now? She glanced out the window, but got no help from the walking dead. She blew her hair out of her face and shook his hand. "Yeah." Oh, she was so going to the Bad Place.

"Why don't you sit down?" Her mother indicated the vacant seat beside Ted.

There wasn't anything else to do but sit. Ted looked just as he had last time she'd seen him, in a button down white shirt and a tie. Maybe the tie had changed. She probably looked a fright sitting next to him, in her sweaty workout clothes, her hair a mess.

She fiddled with her hands as Reverend Joseph cleared his throat. "Well, there's no point in beating around the bush. Your mother tells me you're getting married, and that she's worried about the two of you."

Ted tugged on his collar, but said nothing. Sidney squirmed. "We're fine," was all she managed to squeak out.

Reverend Joseph nodded, a knowing look on his face. "You're both young."

Sidney picked that up and ran with it. "Yes! We're young. In fact, we haven't set a date yet because we want to take things slow."

Ted nodded and grabbed her hand. "We aren't going to rush into anything."

Sidney's mother frowned, obviously not pleased by this. Reverend Joseph, on the other hand, smiled and leaned forward. "I think this is a good idea."

Her mother clicked her tongue against her teeth. "But, waiting too long can be—"

"Phyllis," the reverend interrupted. "They need to go at their own pace. You wouldn't want them to rush into anything and then regret the decision later." He turned back to the two of them. "Now, let's set up a time when you can come in and talk. I'd like to go over a few things with you two that I think would be helpful."

Sidney swallowed the lump forming in her throat. She forced herself to speak. "Sure." Anything to get them out of there.

Her mother gripped the arms of her chair. "But Reverend, do you think it's wise for Sidney to be spending so much time with another man?"

Heat climbed her face. "He's a client, Mom."

"I'm sure Sidney can make those decisions on her own," her father said, looking mortified.

The front door swung open and Natalie walked in. She froze when she saw everyone sitting in the living room. "What's going on?"

Ted loosened his tie. Her mother stood. "We're just talking with Reverend Joseph. Do you want to pull up a seat?"

Natalie's gaze bounced from Ted, to Sidney, to the Reverend. "Um…no."

Sidney saw an opportunity to get out of there, and stood. "Well, thank you for coming over tonight, Reverend. It was wonderful to speak to you. I look forward to talking with you in the future." She tugged on Ted's arm and he stood as well. "We'd better be going."

"Of course." Reverend Joseph's wide smile came back. "I'll call you."

"Yes! You do that." Sidney practically dragged Ted to the door, looping her arm through his. "I'll see you guys later!" They were outside before anyone could object.

Sidney shoved Ted over to his car. The sun had set and darkness surrounded them. She whispered, "Can I have a ride home?"

"Sure. No problem." He smiled at her.

As soon as they were in the car, Sidney turned to him. "I'm so sorry! I'll get you out of this soon, I promise."

He shrugged. "I actually don't mind. I like your family." A hint of a smile played on his lips, but she had no idea why.

When they were down the street, he cast a sideways glance at her. "You okay?"

She turned up the air conditioning and pointed the vent at her face. "Other than being completely embarrassed by my mother, I'm fine."

"I thought you handled it well." His face sobered. "What's going on with you and Blake, anyway?"

"Nothing!" She blew out a breath in frustration. That wasn't exactly true, at least not if she counted her stupid crush. But that didn't count, because Blake wasn't serious about her. "He's just a friend. And a client. I'm setting him up with other women, for heaven's sake. You'd think my mother would get that."

Ted pulled into her parking lot and killed the engine. "Well, you can't blame her. You're always with him." Ted got out of the car before she could stop him, and he came around and opened her door.

"It's not like I go out of my way to see him. Blake has a way of just showing up."

Ted helped her out of the car and walked to her front door. "Then maybe he's trying to tell you something."

What was he implying? That Blake liked her as more than just a friend? That was ridiculous. She snorted. "Yeah, right. Blake's too much of a flirt to get serious."

Ted's eyebrows rose, but he didn't say anything.

She pulled him into a hug. "Thanks for once again covering for me tonight. I really appreciate it."

A pair of headlights shone on them as a truck pulled into the parking lot. It looked a lot like Blake's truck. He was done with his date. How long had he been with Angie? It was getting late. Had they hit it off? Was he coming to tell her he had found his match?

Sidney's heart pounded, and she impulsively whispered, "Help me out a little, will you?" Then she mashed her lips to Ted's. He tried to pull back, but she wrapped her arms around him and held on. It was the most awkward kiss she'd ever experienced, with neither one of them moving their lips. He stood, frozen, and she didn't want to let go because Blake might have hit it off with Angie. Now, she realized that didn't make a lot of sense, but for some reason, kissing Ted felt like the best thing to do.

A car door slammed and Sidney pulled back and smiled at Ted. "Thank you, again."

He blinked, his eyes growing wider by the second. "Um…"

Blake walked up to them and folded his arms across his chest, a scowl on his face. "Ted." He nodded a curt greeting.

Ted looked like he was going to faint. "Blake."

The two men stared each other down for a moment. Then Ted hitched up his pants and said, "I guess you two have some business to discuss."

"Yes," Blake said, and planted his feet apart.

"I'll just be going then." He gave Sidney a half-hearted wave. "We'll get together later and…plan the wedding…or something."

Sidney almost burst into laughter, but she held it together. "Okay, then."

Ted climbed into his car and they watched him drive off. Blake's scowl deepened. "You were out with Ted tonight?"

"Yes. What's wrong with that? He's my fiancé." Maybe Blake wouldn't notice she was in running gear, her phone strapped to her arm, while Ted was wearing business clothes.

"Nothing." Blake stared down the street where Ted's smart car had disappeared.

Sidney pulled out her keys, but waited for Blake to say something. She didn't want to imply she was inviting him in by opening the door. When he just stood there staring off into space, she said, "What did you need?"

He turned to her. "Just wanted to give you a report on my date."

Her stomach clenched, but she ignored it. "You know, you can just email me to let me know how it went. You don't have to come over after each date."

"You're right," he said almost to himself. "I should go."

He looked so deflated that she suddenly felt bad for forcing him out. She sighed. "No, it's okay. Come in. Let's talk about how it went." She unlocked her door and ushered him inside.

CHAPTER 16

Blake was an utter mess, and he knew it. When he saw Sidney kissing Ted, he'd almost gone insane. The urge to punch the guy had overcome him, and he'd had to fold his arms in order to control himself. What was Sidney doing? She was carrying the lie too far.

Unless...

Was it possible the lie had become real somehow? Like in the romance novel on Sidney's coffee table, had she fallen in love with her pretend fiancé? The thought made him curse himself for his idea to wait and see if she'd tell him the truth.

What if she'd fallen for Ted? And why did that thought make him want to punch something?

Sidney plopped down on the couch and waited for him to sit beside her. "Now, how did it go? Do you want to date Angie again?" Her eyes were wide with curiosity.

He'd forgotten all about the date. What should he say? That it was unremarkable? Angie was nice, but there weren't any sparks there. Of course there weren't. He'd been thinking about Sidney the whole time. He definitely wasn't going to tell her that!

What was wrong with him? Sidney was either falling in love with Ted, or she was lying about being with him as an excuse so he would leave her alone. Either way, she wasn't interested. He should take the hint and move on.

Sidney whacked his leg, pulling him out of his thoughts. "Are you going to talk or just sit there?"

"Yes. I mean, the date went well."

Sidney stared at him. "That's it? It went well?"

She seemed bothered by this, and he wondered what was up. And then words just started spilling out of his mouth. "Yes, quite well actually. I think Angie's pretty amazing."

Why had he said that? What was this, high school? Was he trying to make Sidney jealous? How very mature of him. He mentally smacked himself.

"Well..." Sidney blinked, a bit speechless. "That's great."

"I'm taking her back out tomorrow." Lie. Why were these words coming out of his mouth?

"Would you like to put your service on hold, then, while you explore things with Angie?" She fiddled with the quilt hanging over the back of her couch, not looking him in the eye.

And then he saw it. The out he needed. If he said he was dating Angie, Sidney wouldn't match him up with anyone else. Perfect! "Yes, please put it on hold."

"Okay."

They both sat in silence for a few moments, neither one looking at the other, which was stupid. She didn't want him there. Why was he still sitting on her couch?

He stood. "I guess that's about it."

"All righty, then." She looked like she had just swallowed a bug. "Let me know if you change your mind and want another match." She opened the front door.

He didn't want to leave, but there wasn't anything else to

do. "I will," he said, his chest suddenly feeling heavy. He stepped outside to the sound of crickets chirping.

"Bye." She shut the door and he just stood there looking at it awhile, unsure of what had gone wrong. He'd wanted to come tell her about his date—how Angie talked too much, and laughed too loud. He'd meant to suggest they bring out the vanilla ice cream he'd seen in her freezer. Maybe play a little Scrabble.

Instead, he'd caught her kissing Ted.

He climbed into his truck and backed out of his parking space. Maybe it was best to make Sidney think he and Angie had hit it off. He needed to stop this obsession he had. Sidney wasn't going to open up to him, and he wasn't going to force her to want to.

It was best to try to forget about the whole thing.

~

Sidney watched Blake's taillights fade, then let the living room window curtain fall back in place and went into the kitchen. Blake and Angie had hit it off. Of course. Angie was a sweetheart, and Blake was…Blake. Who wouldn't like him?

She grabbed a glass from her dishwasher and turned on the faucet, letting it run cold before filling the glass. It was okay that he and Angie liked each other. That'd mean he'd come around less. Maybe she could finally think, without him hovering all the time.

The water wasn't very cold, but it cooled her off and quenched her thirst. She needed a shower before bed. Maybe she'd read, instead of going right to sleep. She had nothing scheduled tomorrow and was planning on sleeping in, anyway.

Her phone dinged and she pulled it out.

Phyllis: *Grayson is flying in for a visit next Saturday. I was thinking we should have a family cookout in the backyard. Can you and Ted make it? 6:00pm.*

Sidney's heart soared. Grayson was coming! She texted back.

Sidney: *I'll ask.*

She texted Ted to make sure he didn't mind attending another family event. His message came right back.

Ted: *Sounds fun. I'll pick you up at six.*

She sent a confirmation message to her mother and was on cloud nine the rest of the evening. She hadn't seen Grayson in so long. She couldn't wait!

~

Sidney stirred the macaroni salad while listening to her favorite playlist on her phone. She sang along as One Direction belted out a love song in three-part harmony. Her brother's plane would land in a few hours and her heart wouldn't stop pounding.

She and Grayson had been close growing up, which might have seemed weird since she was the youngest and he was the oldest, but she and Natalie had never bonded like that. Maybe because she and Grayson had more in common. They both liked sports and outdoor activities, and Natalie never wanted to do anything but go shopping.

The salad looked good, so she snapped on the lid and placed it in the refrigerator. She had so much pent-up energy, she decided to put on her running shoes and take another jog before getting ready for the party.

As she suspected, now that Blake had a girl, he'd stopped coming around. Half of her felt relief. She didn't have that constant reminder of her crush, and her humiliation. But the other half of her missed him, which she hated.

Why would she miss him when all he did was flirt and mess with her head? She had hated seeing him flirt with Natalie, but she hated it even more when he turned his charm her way. And that kiss? No man should be allowed to kiss like that.

She jogged down the sidewalk and tried to push all thoughts of Blake out of her head. She wouldn't have to see him anymore. She could concentrate on something else. The hot sun beat down on her, and she turned up her music.

After her run, she showered and got dressed. By the time Ted arrived, she was in a better mood. All thoughts of Blake had left. Pretty much. She grabbed her salad and slid into Ted's car.

As he drove, she related funny Grayson stories. He looked over at her and grinned. "You really miss him, don't you?"

"Yes. I can't believe it's been three years."

Ted parked the car. "Well, you don't have to wait a minute longer." He nodded toward the front yard.

Grayson stood there talking with her father. She handed Ted the salad and bolted out of the car. She ran to Grayson and squealed when he picked her up for a hug, swinging her around in a circle. "Sidney. How are you?"

Grayson's sandy-blond hair hung in his eyes. He'd gained a little weight since the last time she saw him, and he sported a goatee which made him look ten years older. "I'm good," she said. She turned around and motioned to Ted, now walking up to them with the salad bowl. "Grayson, this is Ted. Ted, my brother Grayson."

Her brother smiled and extended his hand to Ted. "Nice to meet you." He turned back to her and his smile widened. "Mom says you're engaged. Congratulations, although I have to admit, I always thought you'd marry Blake."

Sidney sucked in a quick breath and then started coughing. "You what?" she choked.

Grayson laughed. "You were always head over heels for him. I was sure someday he'd wake up and realize you two were perfect for each other."

"Who's perfect for each other?" Blake's voice came from behind her.

Sidney spun around so fast she knocked into Ted, who seemed to be enjoying the conversation, based on the grin on his face. "No one," she just about shouted, while desperately trying not to blush. What was Blake doing here?

Grayson muttered, "Speak of the devil." Then he smiled and gave Blake a hug. "I'm so glad you could join us. It's been forever."

"Too long," Blake said, patting Grayson on the back.

Sidney swallowed the hard lump in her throat. Of course Blake would be invited. He and Grayson had been best buds. She should have prepared herself.

Natalie pulled up in her little red Toyota. Grayson left the group to go greet her, and their father excused himself to go check on the grill. Blake nodded at her and Ted and then left to join Grayson.

Ted clasped her hand. "You didn't expect Blake to be here, did you?" He offered her a kind smile.

"No, but it's okay. Like I said, there's nothing between us."

Ted didn't look like he believed her, but said nothing.

"We should go out back." Sidney took the pasta salad from Ted and led him through the house and out the patio door.

Her father stood at the grill flipping the hamburgers. When he glanced at them, he smiled. "How are the two love birds?"

Was this how the whole night was going to go? "Just fine, Dad."

Sidney set the pasta salad on the serving table and lifted off the lid. At least the heat wasn't so bad today. And she couldn't wait to hear all about what Grayson had been up to.

Soon everyone came into the backyard and they sat around the long table her father had set up. Sidney ended up sitting across from Grayson. Natalie sat between Grayson and Blake. They didn't have enough plastic outdoor chairs, so Ted ended up sitting in a folding lawn chair on the end of the table. He didn't seem to mind.

Natalie cozied up to Blake. "What have you been up to?" She batted her eyelids.

"I've been dating Angie Nicholson."

"Oh." Natalie's face fell, and she folded her hands in her lap.

Sidney knew how she felt. Every time she thought about Blake and Angie, it was like her insides were being eaten by acid. She just needed to think about something else.

After her father said grace, Sidney kicked her brother under the table. "What's it like writing for a show like Forensic Science?"

"It's cool getting to be a part of it. The team I work with is great. And the best part is, I sometimes get to be on set. You know, where Ally Young is working." He raised his eyebrows up and down.

"Shut up!" She whacked him on the arm with the back of her hand. "You don't stand a chance with her. She's a TV star. You're...you."

"I'll have you know, Ally and I have this thing going." He put on a smug smile.

Natalie gaped at him. "You're dating Ally Young?"

"Well, not exactly dating." He picked up his hamburger. "You see, we do this thing where I pretend not to stare at her on set, and she pretends not to notice me."

Natalie laughed, and Grayson joined in.

Ted pointed to the trees just past their backyard. "Are

these the famous 'woods' you talk about? Where you and Grayson used to explore as kids?"

Sidney nodded. "Yes. We'd explore in there for hours." She took a sip of her lemonade and then pointed. "You see that path? If you follow that about a quarter mile, it forks to the left and the right. If you go right, you'll eventually come to a bridge spanning the river."

Grayson wiped his face with his napkin. "Dad told us to never go to the left, because we'd hit quicksand. It wasn't until I was a teenager that I realized he was pulling our legs."

"What?" Sidney shrieked. "That was a lie?"

Everyone at the table laughed, and Sidney felt her face grow hot. She'd totally believed her father. How was she to know he was joking? Thinking about it now, it seemed ridiculous that there'd be quicksand in Bishop Falls. She'd just never stopped to think about it until now.

"Dad!" Grayson called out. "Sidney just now found out you were kidding about the quicksand."

Her father leaned forward and stared at them. "What quicksand?"

"Remember when you told us not to go left, because of the quicksand?" Grayson asked.

"I did?" He blinked.

Sidney couldn't believe it. "You mean I spent years avoiding that path in the woods because you were trying to be funny, and now you don't even remember it?"

Blake ducked his head so she wouldn't see him laughing. But soon it didn't matter because the whole table burst into laughter.

Ted, probably trying to take the spotlight off her, spoke up. "Natalie, what have you been up to lately?"

Natalie smiled, and it wasn't a flirty smile like she usually had on. It was more genuine. "I got a new job."

"You did?" Grayson asked. "Where are you working now?"

"At the animal shelter."

"I thought they only took volunteers," Sidney said.

Natalie's cheeks flushed pink. "They do have a few paid positions. I've been volunteering there for two years, and when one of the staff left, they asked me to apply."

"That's great," Ted said, smiling at her. "I didn't know you volunteered."

Sidney didn't know it either. In fact, it was so unlike Natalie to do something for someone else, she was speechless.

Natalie's face brightened and she turned to Ted. "I love working with the animals. It's priceless when a family comes in and we're able to help find them a forever pet they can take care of and love."

Ted continued to smile at Natalie, and Sidney wondered why her sister was acting so different. She wasn't her brazen, flirty self. Maybe she was still pouting about Blake dating Angie.

Gah. Why had she thought about them again, to torture herself?

As they ate, Sidney and Grayson laughed about old times, and she did her best to ignore the hole in her chest that opened up whenever she thought about Blake and his new love interest.

CHAPTER 17

Blake helped Phyllis clean off the table. He couldn't quite let Sidney out of his line of sight, even though it was obvious she didn't want to talk to him. Didn't want him there. Not that she'd been rude to him. Just more like an uncomfortable shift in their relationship. He'd thought about not coming, but Grayson had been his best friend as a kid, and he wanted to see him again. Plus, if he were being honest with himself, he wanted to see Sidney again, too.

He'd spent the week flip-flopping between feeling relief that he didn't have to be set up with anyone else, and beating himself up over lying to Sidney. He hated seeing her with Ted and didn't know whether her affection for him was real or fake. And he hated that they couldn't just be honest with each other.

Ted sat on a lounge chair next to Natalie. They seemed to be in deep conversation, but he wasn't sure what they'd have to talk about. Sidney was chatting with Grayson. Phyllis went inside to get a wet rag, so Blake wandered over to where Grayson and Sidney were talking.

Sidney didn't notice him at first. "And then you ate it! I thought Blake was going to throw up!" She and Grayson laughed.

Blake made a face. "Are you talking about that worm?"

They turned to him. Grayson nodded. "Yeah. Your face was so green."

"Dude, you ate a worm!" Blake said.

Sidney punched him in the arm. "You dared him to."

"I didn't think he'd do it!"

Sidney busted out laughing, and suddenly the awkwardness was gone. It was like it used to be. They talked for a while, remembering old times. When the conversation lagged, Blake walked over to the table and snagged a cup of lemonade.

When he turned back around, Sidney had vanished. A flash of white T-shirt darted through the trees just beyond the trail into the woods, and he knew where she was going.

He casually walked through the backyard, then started down the trail. He followed the flashes of white down the twisty path until he came to the fork in the road. Just as he thought, she'd gone left. She'd always been an explorer at heart. He grinned and followed after her.

He didn't really know why he was following her, other than his stupid instinct to be near her. He tried telling himself it was to protect her…that she shouldn't be alone in the woods this close to sundown, but that was a lie. These woods were safe. He just really wanted to be with her.

The trail twisted for a while, then came to a clearing. He found Sidney sitting on a log that lay next to the riverbank. She was simply sitting there, looking at the river, and the scene seemed so peaceful he hated to interrupt her thoughts. But he couldn't stand there and watch her without letting her know he was there. He cleared his throat.

She turned, startled. "Oh, it's you." She faced the river again, turning her back on him.

Oops. She was mad at him. "Sorry. I probably shouldn't have followed you."

She sighed. "No, it's okay." She scooted over. "Have a seat." She picked a weed and twisted it through her fingers.

He sat beside her and they watched the sun dip below the tree line. The sky was alight with bright oranges and pinks. They were silent for a few minutes, as nature gave them a show. Dusk settled in, and he turned to look at her.

Tears streamed down her cheeks, and his stomach clenched. "What's wrong?"

She wiped her face with the back of her hand. "Nothing. It's stupid." She tossed the mangled weed on the ground and smiled despite her watery eyes.

"Are you upset with me?" he asked, his voice quiet. The last thing he wanted to do was cause her any distress. "I can go…"

She shook her head. "No."

His throat constricted as he watched her blink back more tears. She seemed to struggle with what to say, so he stayed silent. He wanted to put his arm around her…to pull her close, but he refrained.

Finally, she spoke. "I just miss the way things used to be, you know? Everything changes." She looked out at the river. "We're not the same."

He let her words sit in the air for a minute. He understood. It would never be like it used to be when they were kids. "I know."

She wiped at her cheeks again. "It's stupid. I know people grow up. We get our own lives. Grayson loves what he's doing. And you…" Her sentence trailed off.

What did she mean, and him? What had he done? He

waited for her to continue, but she didn't. After a moment, he decided to ask. "And me?"

She smiled at him, although her eyes remained sad. "You're fulfilling your dreams. And that's how it should be."

Blake didn't understand. What did his job have to do with it? He touched her hand, tentatively, and when she didn't pull away, he picked it up and laced his fingers through. "What do you mean?"

~

Sidney could have slapped herself. Why had she mentioned Blake? She should have said she missed Grayson and how that was why she was crying, end of story. But no. She'd had to stick her foot in her mouth.

Now what was she supposed to say, 'You're with Angie now, and I feel like my heart is being ripped apart'? That would go over well. She was supposed to be engaged to Ted.

And now with Blake holding her hand, her pulse was going crazy. Why did she have to let the tears fall? She should have sat there with him, watched the sun set, and ignored her broken heart.

She looked across the river. "I just miss the way things used to be."

He nodded. "We were young and carefree."

It was okay with her if he thought she was upset about the loss of her childhood. "Yes."

He reached up and brushed a tear from her cheek. She leaned into his hand. She couldn't help it. She closed her eyes and soaked in the amazing feel of his touch. His hands were a little rough. The hands of a man who worked hard. Who wasn't afraid of getting in there and getting things done.

The feel of his lips on her forehead created an ache in her chest. She shouldn't let him kiss her, yet she was powerless to stop him. It wasn't a kiss of desire, anyway. It was a comforting gesture.

She pulled back and looked into his blue eyes, and it hit her. She loved him. She'd tried so hard to put up boundaries, to stay away from him...but it wasn't working. She'd fallen in love with Blake. Or maybe she'd always been in love with him, and her heart was just remembering why. He was a good man. Kindhearted. But he wasn't hers.

He never was.

The truth of it made her turn away, and she broke contact with him, folding her hands in her lap. "Why didn't you ever say anything about you and Natalie?" Oh, no. Why had she said that?

"What?" He sounded surprised. "What do you mean, me and Natalie?"

She couldn't back out now. Her mouth had started it, and now she had to finish it. "When we were kids."

"There was no 'me and Natalie' when we were kids. I thought she was hot. That's it."

She shot him a glare. "Really? Sneaking away to kiss her behind the trees didn't mean anything to you?"

His eyebrows shot up. "I kissed Natalie when I was in kindergarten. Grayson dared me. It was one peck, and Natalie started crying and ran inside. She was...like four years old."

"Are you serious?" Sidney couldn't believe it. "You mean..."

Blake laughed, and it echoed across the river. "You thought Natalie was talking about when we were teenagers? Unlikely. She ignored me until we were in college."

Sidney tried to assimilate the information. Blake hadn't been kissing Natalie all along.

Blake continued. "In fact, it wasn't until recently that she started really flirting. I mean, you saw her. Sitting on my lap." He rolled his eyes.

"Yes." Sidney's head spun. Natalie had been crawling all over him...and Blake hadn't wanted her to?

"I think it's good she's gotten a job at the animal shelter."

His words barely registered as Sidney tried to figure out what this new information meant. "I think so, too."

"She seems happier."

Blake had nailed it. Natalie was happy. Sidney hadn't thought about it before. Natalie usually acted bold, but it always seemed superficial with her. Today, she was more genuine. Maybe because the two men at the table were both taken. "Huh. I think you're right."

A breeze picked up and Sidney rubbed her arms. With the sun down, it had gotten a little chilly. "We'd better head back."

"Yes. They'll wonder where we went."

She rose from the log. "I told Grayson where I was going."

"You did?" He stood and stepped over the makeshift seat, taking her hand and helping her over. She let go quickly, because his touch was making her crazy.

She snickered. "Yes. What did you do, just sneak off?"

He coughed into his fist. "Sort of."

Man, he was handsome. She laughed and punched his arm. "You dweeb."

She tried to keep the conversation light as they walked back. She'd had enough heart wrenching for the evening. And even though she kept her demeanor happy, she was trying not to dwell on the fact that Blake had more substance than she'd given him credit for.

But because she'd pushed him away, he was now dating Angie.

CHAPTER 18

Ted helped Sidney's family pull the backyard chairs around the fire pit. The evening had been going well, as far as he could tell. Sidney and Blake had been gone a while, and Phyllis kept wringing her hands and looking at the trees. Natalie was inside the house, gathering up s'mores ingredients. Doug excused himself to use the restroom.

Phyllis turned to Ted. "I'm so sorry. I don't know what's gotten into her. Sidney should be here, with you. How rude of her to leave you like this."

He waved his hand. "It's fine."

"No, it's not." Her face was full of worry. "She's being totally inappropriate."

Guilt filled Ted. He didn't want Phyllis to think her daughter was treating him poorly. But what could he do about it?

Grayson approached them. "What's going on?"

Phyllis scoffed. "Sidney. She's off with Blake again." She motioned toward the trees.

Grayson rubbed his goatee. "What do you mean, again?"

"She's always with Blake. Ever since he came back. It's just not right when you're engaged to another man."

Grayson turned to Ted, a scrutinizing look on his face. "When did you two get engaged?"

When was it? Crud. He didn't remember. "A few weeks ago."

"And when's the wedding?"

Ted stuck his hands in his pockets, glad he had an answer for this one. "We're taking things slow."

Grayson narrowed his eyes. "Uh, huh. And how did you meet?"

Ted tugged at his shirt collar. It suddenly was too tight. "Through my sister."

"What, at a party?"

"No. Just...through my sister." Oh, this was not going well.

Grayson crossed his arms over his chest. "You're not really engaged, are you?"

What? Where had that come from? His forehead grew impossibly hot and he wiped at the sweat forming there. Phyllis glared at him.

"What do you mean, not engaged?" Phyllis said.

Grayson chuckled. "Oh my gosh, I can't believe it. She's totally faking it."

Ted panicked. What should he do? Confess, or deny it? He swallowed, trying to give himself time to think. "Um..."

Grayson put his arm around Ted's shoulders. "What's the deal? Why are you guys telling everyone you're engaged?"

Phyllis looked like her head was going to explode. "What are you saying?"

Grayson turned to her. "Mom, it's okay. Let Ted talk."

Great. Now they were looking at him. "We...uh..." There was no more stalling. He had to say something. "She needed a fiancé to help her business."

"How does that help?"

He tugged at his collar again. "I guess people didn't believe she could match them…since she was single."

Grayson nodded. "And why didn't she just pick Blake?"

"I don't know." He really didn't know the answer to that one. "She keeps saying there's nothing between them."

"She does?" Grayson put his hands behind his back, thinking. "Why would she say that? She's been in love with him for years."

Phyllis, who had looked like she was going to murder someone, suddenly cooled. "She's in love with Blake?"

"Of course, Mom. Didn't you notice?"

Phyllis's cheeks reddened. "I noticed, but I thought she was engaged to Ted! I called Reverend Joseph over to the house!"

Grayson burst out laughing. "That's great, Mom."

The patio door opened, and Natalie emerged. Heat crept up Ted's face. "Listen, you can't say anything, okay?"

Phyllis smoothed out her dress. "Well, I certainly won't."

Grayson chuckled. "Oh, man," he said under his breath.

Ted shot him a look, and Grayson raised his hands. "I promise."

Natalie set the things she'd gathered down on the table. "What are you guys huddled together for?"

Grayson backed up, and Phyllis walked over to the table to fuss with how the chocolate was displayed. "No reason, dear."

Natalie grabbed a roasting stick. "Then let's roast some marshmallows."

~

When Sidney got back to the yard, her family was sitting around the fire pit, talking. Natalie and Ted were in conversation, both holding marshmallows over the fire. A table occupying all the items needed for s'mores sat nearby. Grayson turned to Sidney. "Have a nice walk?"

He had a smirk on his face, and she didn't quite know how to interpret it. "Yes." Was he going to make another crack about the quicksand?

Grayson didn't say anything else, just motioned to the two empty chairs and she and Blake sat down. "Want to roast a marshmallow?"

Sidney shrugged. "Sure."

Grayson reached to the small table behind him and tossed her the bag, and then handed her a long stick. "You?" he asked Blake.

"Of course. What's a backyard fire without s'mores?"

She snickered. "Just don't burn your marshmallow." She stuck one on her stick, and placed it above the fire.

Blake's grin stretched across his face. "I don't know what it is. I can't ever just toast one. Mine always catch on fire." He nudged her. "But yours turn out perfect."

"It takes skill." She gave him a smug smile.

He rolled his eyes. "Yeah, right. Luck, maybe."

"We'll see who has the perfect marshmallow."

Grayson snorted. "The perfect marshmallow? Not this again."

"She's right," Blake said. "Sidney always makes the perfect marshmallow."

"Here's a trick." Sidney raised his stick an inch. "Don't put it so close to the fire."

"But then it never cooks."

"You're too impatient. You have to wait for the good things in life." Sidney shot him a cheesy grin.

"But some things are too hard to wait for." Blake shot her back a look.

Grayson moaned and got up from his chair. "I…just can't." He walked into the house.

Sidney turned to Blake. "What was that about?"

He shrugged. "Beats me."

CHAPTER 19

Sidney climbed into Ted's car and Ted shut the door. After he slid into the driver's seat, she said, "That went well, I think."

Ted bit his lower lip and put his car into drive.

She didn't need Spidey senses to see something was wrong. "Ted?"

He glanced at her as he drove. "I'm sorry."

Her stomach churned and she began to sweat. "What are you sorry for? What happened?"

"It wasn't exactly my fault. Grayson figured it out."

Oh, no no no. This couldn't be happening. "Grayson knows we're not engaged?" She tried to keep her voice down from screeching level.

"And your mom. But that's it." He peered at her, cringing a little, like he was afraid she was going to clobber him.

"Oh, I am so dead." She sank down in her seat. "Did she scream? She didn't cuss, did she? Oh, if she did I'm sooo—"

"No. She took it rather well, actually."

Wait...what? "*My* mother? She wasn't upset?"

"She was, at first. But Grayson settled her down. I think

they're happy to know the truth." He looked over at her, like he was hoping she wouldn't yell at him.

Sidney took a deep breath, and let it out slowly. "Okay, then. This is manageable." Her mind began working through what she needed to do. "I need to talk to them and get them to go along with it just for a little while..."

Ted slowed for a stop sign. "If your mother already knows, maybe it's best to come clean. Just rip it off like a Band-Aid and tell everyone."

Her breath caught. Then Blake would know she'd lied to him. "Oh, no. I couldn't."

"Why not? You weren't expecting to carry on this lie forever, were you?"

"No...I thought..." What did she think? Maybe that was her trouble. She wasn't thinking. She'd jumped into this lie to help her business, but it wasn't about that anymore. If she were honest with herself, then she would have to admit it hadn't been about that for a long time.

She was using the lie to keep Blake away. To shield her heart from falling again. But it hadn't worked. And now she had to give up the lie.

She let out a breath. "I don't know what I thought."

Ted gave her a sympathetic look. "You have to tell him."

She stared at Ted. "What are you talking about?"

"Blake. You have to tell him you love him."

She gaped. "I...When did...How did you..."

"Come on, it's obvious. You deny it, but your actions say otherwise."

Great. If Ted could see it, that must mean everyone else could too. Now, instead of her own private humiliation, she would get to live out a very public one. She was in love with a guy who she set up with someone else through her own matchmaking service. She covered her face with her hands and moaned. "That figures."

"It's not so bad," Ted said. "Your mother already knows, and she was the hard one, right? Now all you have to do is tell Blake."

She nodded. "You're right. Of course you are." It was the logical thing to do. The right thing to do.

Then why did she feel a sudden panic clawing its way through her?

~

Sidney pulled her car up to Blake's house and put it in park. She could do this. Right? She had to. Ted was right. Just rip off the Band-Aid.

The morning was cool and his lawn was still wet with dew. Was he up yet? She checked her watch. Nine o'clock. That wasn't too early, was it? She stopped on the sidewalk, clutching her purse, unsure if she should continue to his house or come back later. Maybe after lunch would be better.

No. She needed to do this now. Gathering up her courage, she strode up his front walkway and onto the porch. She pressed the doorbell before she could talk herself out of it.

Blake came to the door in a T-shirt and a pair of worn jeans with splotches of paint on them. His eyebrows rose when he saw it was her. "Sidney?"

"Sorry, I didn't mean to interrupt. You look like you're in the middle of something."

"I was, but it can wait." He stepped to the side. "Do you want to come in?"

Say no. Say no. "Sure." Gah. Why didn't she listen to her inner voice? She walked into his living room and took a look around. "Kind of sparse in here, isn't it?"

Blake chuckled. "I'm not all the way unpacked yet."

"What?" She whacked him in the chest. "It's been like a whole month since you moved in."

"I know. I'm a slacker. Please, sit." He motioned to the leather couch. Besides that, there was one end table and a lamp. A fireplace took up part of one wall, and a large screen TV hung above the mantle, but the rest of the room was bare.

She sat on the very edge of the couch, to maybe give herself a nice quick exit after she spilled her guts. Nerves shot through her and she swallowed.

Blake plopped down and stretched his arms over the back of the couch. He looked like he belonged there. "What can I do for you?"

Oh no. Now it was time for her to talk, and her mouth was too dry. Her insides quivered. She couldn't do this. "Nothing...I just...wanted to talk."

A curious look overtook his face. "Go for it."

"Ted and I..." Her throat closed and she couldn't breathe. Couldn't make a sound. Okay, the Band-Aid didn't want to come off. It was stuck to her skin. Pulling fast wasn't working. He was sitting there staring at her, and she couldn't tell him. The words wouldn't come out. How was she supposed to tell him she lied about Ted, oh, and by the way, she'd fallen in love with him?

No. That wasn't going to happen. And her lungs needed air. Now. "We broke up," she said, forcing it out. She sucked in air, and tried not to pass out on his floor.

Blake's eyes widened, and he leaned forward. "I'm so sorry."

"It's okay. We were having problems." Guilt wormed its way through her at how easily the lie came off her lips. "I think it's for the better."

He looked at her thoughtfully. "So, now what?"

"I go back to being single I guess."

"You're still wearing your ring."

"Right." Crud. She'd forgotten to take it off. "I meant to give it back…to Ted." She wiggled it off her finger and stared at it. "Guess I have to do that still."

Blake sat silent while she put the ring in her purse. She didn't know what else to say. Telling him she was in love with him was out. Totally. That Band-Aid was stuck fast, and not coming off. Ever.

The silence was getting awkward, so she stood. "Okay, well, that's all. I better be going."

Blake hopped up off the couch. "Wait. There's nothing else you want to say?"

"What else did you want me to say?" Panic ripped through her.

He rubbed his forehead. "Nothing." He raked his hand through his hair and then smiled. "Since you're here, want to help me with something?"

What did that mean? "Sure," she said tentatively.

He led her through the dining room and into the kitchen. The walls were taped and painted in primer, and the floor was covered with a drop cloth. "I'm ready to paint, but I can't decide." He held up two paint chips, one a deep red, the other a dark green.

She looked around at his dark cabinets and frowned. "I'd go with a lighter color." She fished through a stack of paint chips and picked one up. "This would look good."

He made a face. "Tan?"

"It's not tan, it's…" She peered at the paint chip. "Caramel Kiss."

"Well, I think I'd like a little more color in here. You know, liven things up a bit." He squinted at her. "You used to like color. I remember you painting your bedroom walls purple."

She laughed, her tension slipping away. She was glad they weren't still talking about her and Ted. "Yes, and it's still purple. If my parents ever want to sell that house, they're going to have to give it a good three or four coats of Caramel Kiss."

"I can't paint my kitchen tan. Any other colors catch your eye?"

She shuffled through the samples and then held up a light blue. "I like this one."

He leaned over her shoulder. "Jamaica Bay. I like that one. Mostly blue, but has a little bit of teal in it."

"I think it would go well with the dark fixtures you have in here."

He nodded. "You're right. Jamaica Bay it is." He grinned at her. "Wanna come to the store with me?"

Her first instinct was to say no, that she had something with Ted, but then she realized she couldn't use Ted as an excuse anymore. "Are you trying to sucker me into helping you paint?"

"Would it work?"

"Only if there's ice cream involved."

"Deal." He turned his full grin on her, which made her heart flip-flop in her chest.

She turned away, unable to bear it. "Okay, let's go."

It didn't take long to get to the store. Blake talked to the paint guy while she walked down the paintbrush aisle. She grabbed a roller and then looked at the brushes. When Blake came around the corner, she held up two different kinds. "This one is cheaper, but this other one will do a better job."

Blake scratched his chin. "Better to spend an extra dollar or two now, and have a better paint job in the end." He took the cheaper one from her and slid it back on the peg hook. She ignored the tingles as their fingers touched.

When the paint was ready, they paid for their items and left the store. Blake drove down the street, staring straight ahead. "Do you mind if I ask what happened, between you and Ted?"

Sidney groaned inwardly. Nice. Now she had to lie some more. Guilt made her stomach turn. "We realized it wasn't working." That was sort of true. It wasn't working, because they weren't really dating…and because Grayson figured it out.

He nodded, still not looking at her. "And what made you come tell me about it?" He clenched his jaw, like he was upset about something.

"I just figured you should know." Did he think she was trying to imply something? She quickly went on. "I mean, not that I think you and me…" She nervously laughed. "You're dating Angie now. So don't get the wrong idea."

He lifted an eyebrow and looked at her. "The wrong idea?"

Gah. Now he wanted her to explain herself? "Yeah. We're just friends. And friends tell each other stuff, right? That's all. I was just…telling you."

Oh, please let that be enough.

He clenched the steering wheel and slowly nodded, staring ahead again. "I see."

He didn't say anything more, and she breathed an internal sigh of relief.

CHAPTER 20

Blake didn't know what was going on. Sidney was abandoning her fake relationship, but was not coming clean about it. She was still holding onto the lie. And to make matters worse, she was still keeping her distance. He wasn't sure why she hadn't simply kept up the pretense of her and Ted. And why had she come all the way over to his house? It didn't make sense. The only thing he could gather was that she wanted to tell him something more, but was too embarrassed.

He pulled into the garage and opened the door for Sidney. Maybe if they spent the day together, she'd open up. They brought the painting supplies into the kitchen. "Here, let me get you something to put on over your shirt. I'm sure you don't want to get paint on your nice clothes."

She shrugged. "Okay."

He went into his bedroom and rummaged through his closet. After he found an old dress shirt that was too tight around his neck, he walked back into the kitchen and tossed it at her. She held it up. "You want me to wear a dress shirt? To paint in?"

"It's too tight. I won't wear it again."

She looked at him like he was a bit crazy, but put the shirt on anyway. The sleeves hung down too long, so she rolled them up.

Man, she looked good in his shirt. He turned away. "That works."

She poured paint into the tray and they both got started in with their brushes. Blake glanced at her as they worked. She was going fast, but her paint was smooth. "You're good. You have a lot of experience painting?"

"Yes. My freshman year I worked for a guy who flipped houses. I mostly painted, but sometimes he had me laying tile or putting up drywall. I learned a lot."

"Impressive."

She smiled. "He paid well, and I enjoyed the work. Sadly, he went out of business after a year, so I had to find another job."

He wanted to keep her talking. She was more relaxed that way. "What did you do then?"

"Don't laugh." She pointed at him.

"That's not fair. You can't tell me I can't laugh, because that makes me think of laughing. Now I have to laugh, no matter what you say."

"Fine." She rolled her eyes. "I was a telemarketer."

He chuckled. "No way."

She dipped her brush into the paint. "I know. It's a terrible job, but it pays well. Even better than painting." She'd covered twice as much as he'd done, in the same amount of time.

"Did you get a lot of angry people on the phone?"

"No, not really. It wasn't so bad. I was an inbound telemarketer, which is the kind you get when you call in to a company. So, I mainly took orders and tried to up-sell people."

"Ah, so you weren't the annoying girl who called at supper time."

She peered at him, her lashes low. "No. I was the annoying girl who took your call to order a handbag, and by the time you got off the phone I'd convinced you to buy the matching coin purse, wallet and shoes."

He smiled. "Ooh, what color purse did I buy?"

"Blue. To match your eyes." The way she'd said it sounded quite flirty, and she blushed.

Blake laughed. "I can see why it paid more than painting. I bet you up-sold quite a bit."

She didn't answer, just focused on her painting while turning a deeper red.

"Looks like we can start with the rollers." He set his paint-brush down and picked up a roller.

She was faster at that, also, and soon they had the entire room painted. Sidney stood back, looking at their work. "You did a good job priming the wall. I don't think we'll need a second coat."

He stood beside her, studying the wall. "I agree."

She turned to him. "It looks nice."

"I'm glad you made me go with the lighter color. Makes the room look bigger." He studied her face. "You've got an eyelash on your cheek."

She closed her eyes. "Get it off."

He brushed her cheek with the pad of his thumb, not realizing he had paint on him until she looked like she was preparing for some tribal war. "Oops."

She opened her eyes. "What?"

He chuckled. "I got some paint on you."

Her mouth dropped open and she turned and bent over to look at her reflection on the toaster. "Oh, you're gonna pay for that." She picked up her brush.

Blake took a step back, his hands up in a defensive move. "It was an accident!"

She smiled, a devilish glint in her eyes. "Hold still, and it won't be so bad."

"I'm not going to hold still while you paint my face."

She came at him fast. Her paintbrush bristles left wet paint on his nose before he caught her wrists. "Ha!" She laughed. "Gotcha."

He tried to turn her own paintbrush on her, but she was too strong. He couldn't get it close enough. So he stepped forward and used his nose to get paint on her other cheek.

"So not fair!" she said, laughing. "You wiped off all yours."

He was suddenly aware of how close he was to her. They were just inches apart, and he could feel her breath on his cheek. It made his heart speed up. He looked into the depths of her brown eyes, and all his playfulness vanished.

He wanted to kiss her, but he knew he couldn't. It wouldn't be right. He couldn't take that intimacy from her. She needed to give it to him.

She sobered. "Okay. I surrender." She let the paintbrush fall to the drop cloth, and she squirmed.

He let her go and turned away. He needed to give up the idea that she was going to open up to him. She was still putting up walls, even if they were no longer named Ted.

~

Sidney took a deep breath as she washed out the paintbrush. Why did Blake have such an effect on her? She really needed to get away from him. Being around him was just more torture on her. If she didn't have the guts to tell him she loved him, then she needed to get out of the way and let him explore a relationship with Angie.

The thought of Blake with Angie made her want to scream. But she'd matched them because they had so many common interests. And they both deserved someone in their life.

Her stomach turned sour, and she looked at Blake. "I'm not feeling well. I'd better head home."

He turned off the faucet and gave her a concerned look. "Are you okay?"

"Yes, I'm fine. I think I'm just tired." She walked into the living room. "I might go home and take a nap."

"All right." He didn't look convinced. "Give me a call later. Let me know how you're doing."

"Okay." *Not gonna happen.* She didn't look him in the eye. Instead, she picked up her purse and headed toward the door. She needed fresh air.

She stepped out onto his porch. "See ya." She hoped she wouldn't. She needed a break from seeing him.

He nodded. "Okay." His eyes held something, but she wasn't quite sure what.

She practically ran to her car and sped home. Once inside, she plopped down onto her living room chair. She looked down and realized she still had Blake's dress shirt on. Dang. She unbuttoned it and tossed it on the coffee table. She'd have to give it back later. Or not.

She snuggled down in her chair, the one perfect for watching TV, and turned on Netflix. Time for a Psych marathon. Shawn and Gus always made her laugh.

But even as the opening song played, she knew it wasn't going to make her feel any better. She'd gone to Blake's house to get everything out in the open, and she'd failed. And the whole thing made her feel miserable.

Two hours later, her phone pinged. She glanced at the screen.

Grayson: *Flying out in the morning. Want to do dinner?*

She smiled and typed out a reply. *Okay. What time?*

Six. I'll pick you up.

Sidney hoped going out with Grayson would improve her mood, but as the time grew closer, her stomach grew worse. By six o'clock, she was feeling like she'd never get out from under the heavy feeling settling inside her.

Grayson pulled up in his rental car. Sidney hopped in, glad to be doing something other than moping around her house. Grayson would be a good distraction.

When he pulled into Sue's parking lot, she groaned. Just what she needed, to be reminded of when she and Blake ate there.

"What?" Grayson said, clearly annoyed. "You love Sue's."

"Sorry. It's fine. I'm just in a bad mood."

Grayson shot her a weird look and got out of the car. After they were seated, he leaned over his menu and cleared his throat. "Okay, spill it."

She stared at him. Was he taking her out just to get more info about her and Ted? That was a low thing to do. She frowned. "Spill what?"

"Everything. I know about Ted, and I know you're in love with Blake, so tell me what's going on."

She pinched her lips together. Did the whole world know? "I guess there's nothing to tell. You apparently already know everything."

Grayson snorted. "Come on. Why are you lying to everyone?"

She folded her arms across her chest and gave him her best glare. She didn't appreciate the ambush. "My business was failing."

He waved his hand dismissively. "You didn't have to tell Mom you were engaged. Why did you?"

She huffed. "If you must know, I did it because I didn't want Blake to find out it was a lie."

"And why did you want Blake to think you were engaged? Did you think he'd find you more desirable that way?"

"That's the stupidest thing I've ever heard."

Grayson looked at her like she had two heads. "Then why?"

The answer was too much to bear, and she blinked back tears. "Because I didn't want Blake to stick around. I didn't want to fall for him again."

The server walked up to their table, smacking on her gum. "Are you ready to order?"

Sidney was too upset to speak, so she ducked her head. Grayson sat forward. "She'll have the cheeseburger meal with a vanilla malt. I'll take the cheese frenchee meal."

"You got it," she said. "Can I have your menus?"

Grayson handed them to her, and she left. Then he placed his hand on Sidney's arm. "What do you mean? You've been in love with him since we were kids."

She sniffed. "I know. Then something happened, and it took me ten years to get over him. I didn't want to do that again."

Grayson looked puzzled. "What happened ten years ago?"

Great. Now she had to tell him. The only positive thing to come out of the whole ordeal was that Blake had never told anyone what had happened. He'd had the decency to keep her humiliation between them. Sidney rubbed her temples and tried to think of a way to say it that wasn't so embarrassing. "I was sixteen."

He nodded, and when she didn't go on, he prodded her. "And?"

"I wanted to show Blake I was interested in him. So I got dressed up, and Leena put makeup on me." She swallowed the lump forming in her throat. "That was the day Blake came for dinner."

Grayson frowned. "Blake was always over for dinner."

She shook her head. "No, he was in college. This was the *last* time he came over for dinner."

Apparently, Grayson didn't remember the event, because he shrugged. "So?"

"So, I flirted all through dinner, and Blake didn't even look at me. He was looking at Natalie."

"She was more his age. You can't blame him."

She stared down at the table. "You're right. But I was young and stupid."

The server came back with their food, and they waited until she was gone to continue.

Grayson picked up his soda and took a sip. "Okay. You flirted and he ignored you. Was that it?"

Sidney shifted in her chair, the seat suddenly uncomfortable. "Unfortunately, no." Did she have to say the next part? Heat crept up her neck, and she blurted it out. "I kissed him."

Grayson choked on his soda. "You what?"

"I know! I can't believe I did it, but as Blake walked by my bedroom, I yanked him inside and planted one on him."

He cringed. "Oh, I bet that didn't go well. What was he, like twenty? You can't blame him for not kissing you back."

"I wish that was all it was." Why was it so hot? It was like a hundred degrees. She picked up a desert menu and fanned her face.

Grayson took a bite of his cheese frenchee. "So, what happened?" He was really getting into the story now.

"He kissed me. Like, really kissed me."

Grayson about choked again. "He did?"

The next part she couldn't say out loud, so she whispered. "He thought I was Natalie."

"Oh no," he said, his face showing his empathy.

"When he found out it was me, he freaked out and left."

"I'm sorry." He put his hand over hers. "I'm sure that was embarrassing."

She nodded. "Yes, but that wasn't the worst part." She blinked more tears away, and her stomach clenched. "He was so disgusted, he never came back."

Grayson shook his head. "No, that's not what happened."

She massaged her forehead. "Yes. That was the last time I saw him, until he came into Blissfully Matched."

"Okay, but he was in college. He was trying to get into medical school." A look of pity filled his face. "He wasn't staying away from you."

She could barely speak over the lump in her throat. "Yes, he was. I know, because he'd come back to Bishop Falls and visit his mother, but he stayed away from me."

"Sidney," Grayson said, his voice low. "He was older than you. He couldn't have dated you."

She looked down at her fingernails. "I know that."

"You can't think he was staying away because of that kiss."

That was exactly what she thought, but she didn't say anything. Instead, she stared at the jukebox sitting in the corner and tried to hold it together.

"Okay. I understand," Grayson said.

She looked at him.

He blew out a breath and leaned back in his chair. "I can see why you lied. You were hurt."

"I was over it."

Grayson looked at her with skepticism. "But you hadn't forgotten."

"True. And I didn't want to get all caught up in my Blake crush again." She stared at her cheeseburger, unable to take a bite. "So I told him I was engaged."

"And when are you going to tell him the truth?"

She froze. "Never."

He plopped the last of his cheese frenchee in his mouth. “That’s real mature.”

She sulked. “I know. But if I tell him I made up the engagement, I’m going to have to tell him why. And I can’t put myself on the line like that. Not again.”

“Then you’re going to lose him.”

“I think I already have,” she whispered.

CHAPTER 21

Sidney stared down at the untouched food on her plate. Grayson nudged her. "You gonna eat that?"

She shook her head and shoved the plate toward him. "No."

He shrugged and picked up the burger. "You really should talk to Mom."

That was the last thing she wanted to do. "Why?"

"Because she's upset that you told her you and Ted were engaged."

Sidney frowned. "Ted says she took it well."

"She didn't scream or murder anyone, if that's what you mean. But she's hurt." He wiped his face with his napkin and stared at her. "Did you really think you'd get away with lying to Mom and never have to face it?"

She sighed and ran her finger along the edge of the table. "I guess I didn't think about it."

"If you don't clear the air between you, it will just get worse."

The door dinged and she glanced over to make sure it wasn't anyone she knew. "I'll talk to her."

Grayson nodded. "Good." He finished eating the rest of her cheeseburger while she watched people come and go, her stomach tightening with each minute. At last he said, "You ready to leave?"

She nodded and stood, grabbing her purse.

After Grayson pulled into her apartment parking lot, they got out and he walked her to her door. "I know it's none of my business, but you really should tell Blake the truth."

She looked down at her shoes. He was probably right, but she didn't think she could bring herself to do it.

Grayson gave her a hug. "Hang in there."

"Have a good flight." She blinked back more tears. Then she socked him in the arm. "And don't forget to call once in a while."

He chuckled. "Okay."

Sidney said goodbye to Grayson and entered her apartment. Natalie was sitting on her couch, her head in her hands, her feet up on the coffee table. A box of tissues sat on the couch beside her. "Natalie? What are you doing here?"

Natalie moaned and put her hands in her lap, revealing the tears streaming down her face. "I'm a horrible person."

Sidney sat down next to Natalie and put her arm around her shoulders, searching for something to say. "It can't be that bad. What happened?"

Natalie plucked a tissue from the box and blew her nose. "It is. It's bad. You're going to hate me."

Sidney clenched her teeth. Had Natalie come on to Blake again? Horrible thoughts pushed their way into her head, and she had to know. "What happened?" she repeated.

"I didn't mean to. It was an accident."

"What did you do?" Her panic was rising. If Natalie didn't tell her, she was going to smack her.

"It was just a kiss, I swear."

Oh no. Natalie kissed Blake. Her gut clenched and she tried not to picture it in her mind. Ugh. Too late. "Tell me what happened," she said, fearing the truth but needing to know.

"Ted came over this morning. He was helping me with some new software."

"Wait…Ted?" Her head spun and relief flooded over her. Her sister hadn't kissed Blake.

"I'm so sorry!" Natalie wailed. "I didn't mean for it to happen. He's just so nice, and he doesn't look at me like other guys. He talks to me like what I think really matters. But I promise, it will never happen again!"

Guilt washed over her, and Sidney bit her lip. "No, it's okay. Ted and I aren't engaged."

Natalie looked at Sidney, her eyes watery. "What?"

"I'm sorry, this is horrible, but Ted and I were never engaged."

Confusion settled on Natalie's face. "You weren't? You mean…you lied?"

"Ted was pretending to be my fiancé to help my business. It was only supposed to be a photo on my desk, but then Mom found out and things got out of hand."

Natalie whacked Sidney's arm. "I can't believe you lied. I felt horrible all day, thinking I'd kissed your fiancé!"

Sidney swallowed, tears threatening to spill over onto her cheeks. "I know. I'm rotten."

Natalie suddenly burst out laughing. "Look at us. We're a mess."

Sidney chuckled and wiped at her eyes. "We are."

"So, you and Ted were never a thing?"

"No."

Natalie put her hand on her chest. "Thank goodness. I thought I was a horrible person for liking him."

Sidney sat back on the couch and put her feet up, mimicking Natalie. "You like him, huh?" She turned to her sister. "Like, like him?"

Natalie nodded. "I think so."

"Wow." Sidney giggled. "What did he do when you kissed him?"

Natalie's eyes grew wide. "He didn't have time to react. I was so mortified that I'd kissed him, I shoved him out the door."

Sidney gasped. "You did what?"

"I know! I need to go talk to him. He must think…" She stood up from the couch. "I'm sorry, I have to go."

"Sure."

Natalie rushed out the door so fast, she didn't close it all the way. Sidney got up from the couch and secured the door. Natalie and Ted? The thought made her head reel. What an unlikely pair.

But she had to admire Natalie, rushing over to Ted's to talk to him and clear things up. That was what she should have done this morning, instead of lying again. Why couldn't she be more like Natalie?

The thought wormed its way around her brain. She wasn't ready to tell Blake, but she needed to face her parents. Grayson was right. She looked at the clock. Nine-thirty. Her parents usually went to bed at ten. Maybe they were still up.

She texted her mother to see if she could come talk.

Phyllis: *We're up. Come on over.*

Nerves assaulted her as she drove to her parents' home. She pulled up in front and cut the engine. This was just something she had to do.

Her mother met her at the door wearing her mumu nightgown. It suited her. "Come in." She ushered her into the living room.

Her father sat on the couch, no expression on his face. Her mother joined him.

Sidney took a seat and wrung her hands. This wasn't going to be easy. She looked at the quilts her mom had spent her life creating, displayed around the room, each one meticulously stitched. There were no shortcuts. She'd spent the hours needed to get them perfect.

"I need to apologize," Sidney said. No one spoke, so she went on. "Ted and I were never engaged, and I shouldn't have lied about it."

Her mother smiled. "We know, dear."

Sidney stared. Who was that, and where did her real mother go? She swallowed nervously. "I'm sorry I lied."

Mom's smile widened. "We know this time of your life can be confusing. You're growing, and things are changing..."

Heat rose to her neck. What was her mother doing, giving her 'the talk?' Sheesh, how old did she think she was? "Hold it, Mom."

Her mother continued, undaunted. "When two people love each other..."

"Mom!" Sidney wanted to sink into the floor. "Ted and I don't love each other."

"Oh, I know, dear."

Her father patted her mother on the knee. "I think it's best if we let Sidney figure things out on her own."

Her mother folded her hands in her lap and nodded. "Very well."

Thank you, heaven above. "I'd better go. I just wanted to apologize." Sidney stood.

Her father came and gave her a hug. "You'll be just fine."

"Thanks, Dad."

When Mom hugged her, she patted her on the back. "You know you can tell us anything. We love you, no matter what."

"I know, Mom."

She left her parents' house, breathing in the cool night air, glad that was over. Now the only person left to talk to was Blake.

Either that, or crawl into bed and never come out again. The latter seemed like a good option.

CHAPTER 22

Sidney clicked through the computer profiles, trying to narrow down a third match for a client, Mickey Phillips. As she clicked, the song Hey Mickey rattled around in her head, and soon she was clicking to the beat. After a minute of that earworm, she turned on the radio. Adele's voice rang out.

Better.

Sidney flipped through a few more profiles until she found herself staring at Angie's face. Why was Angie still listed in with the available profiles? She should have moved her over. Sidney's mouse hovered over the unavailable box, but she didn't click it.

She stared at the phone number. Since she'd been the one who matched Angie and Blake, it wasn't unreasonable for her to call and check up on how things were going, right? She usually left clients alone after they said they'd found a match, but maybe she wasn't being hands-on enough. Maybe it would help her build her business.

Before her head could talk her out of it, she punched up

Angie's number. The line rang three times before someone answered.

"Hello?"

Sidney clenched the phone. "Hi Angie. This is Sidney Reed. How are you doing?"

"I'm fine."

"That's good to hear. Hey, I was just calling as a follow-up. Since Blissfully Matched was the service that matched you up with Blake, I wanted to see how things are going."

"Oh. Well, the date was fun." Her voice sounded chipper. Almost forced.

"I see. And how many dates have you been on with Blake?" Sidney's gut tied in a knot. Did she really want to know this?

"Just the one. Blake's nice and all, but we didn't really mesh."

Sidney stared at the computer screen. "Sorry, I think I misheard you. I thought you said just one."

"Yes, that's right. We only went on the one date."

Sidney's heart pounded in her chest. "You and Blake didn't hit it off?"

"Sidney, are you okay? You sound surprised. I thought Blake would have told you it wasn't a match."

The realization that Blake had lied to her sank in, and her palms began to sweat. "Oh, yes. Sorry. I must have typed it into my computer wrong. I apologize for bothering you."

"It's no bother. Thanks for checking up on the date."

Sidney hung up the phone, her heart in her throat.

Blake had lied. He'd told her he and Angie were dating. But why?

He must have wanted an excuse not to see her again. She thought back to the night he told her. He hadn't come around her place since then.

He was once again running from her. She sat in her chair, too stunned to do anything else. Blake wanted to cut ties.

~

Sidney's week turned into a stressful one. Two clients backed out of their contracts, and she found out her rent was going up. She tried to talk to the landlord about it, but he was evading her. On Friday, she needed some alone time. After work, she ran to the grocery store and bought some chocolate fudge brownie ice cream. It would go really well with a movie on Netflix.

She curled up under the oversized quilt her mother had made for her when she left for college, turned on the television, and dipped her spoon in the carton. The cold felt good on her throat. She scrolled through the movies, avoiding the sappy romantic ones, and selected a nice campy horror.

She was glad she'd changed into her sweats. Much more comfortable while curling up in the chair. She turned off all the lights and watched the movie in the dark. It turned out to be scarier than she'd been thinking. Less campy and more edge-of-your-seat slasher. That's why she screamed when a knock came on her door. She paused the movie.

Her heart hammered in her chest as she stared at the door. Who would be coming over at this hour? She stood, wrapped the quilt around herself, and peeked out the window.

Blake? Not again. She couldn't take any more of him. She leaned up against the door, hoping he'd go away.

Another knock sounded. And then a muffled, "Sidney? Open the door. I know you're home. I heard you scream."

Crud. She slid the lock and opened the door. "What do you want?"

He frowned. "What are you doing in here? Why are the

lights off?" Then he looked at the television. "You're not watching a scary movie, are you? You know you can't handle them."

She stuck out her chin. "I'm not twelve anymore."

He shook his head. "You're right. I'm sorry. Can I come in for a second? I have to get something off my chest."

Oh no. That didn't sound good. "I'd rather you didn't."

He cocked his head to the side and studied her. "Okay. I'll say it here."

She peered out into the creepy darkness and huffed. "Fine. Come in." She yanked him inside and shut the door, then locked it.

He chuckled. "Not afraid of anything out there, are you?"

She flipped on the lights then whacked him in the chest on her way back to her chair. "Shut up." She plopped down with the quilt around her. "What do you want to 'get off your chest?'" she said, making air quotes.

He sat down on the couch, on the side closest to her chair. He looked down at his hands. "I have to tell you something."

She waited for him, and when he didn't go on, she said, "Okay."

He looked up at her, and she was surprised by the intensity in his gaze. "I lied."

That was not what she expected him to say. Her stomach dropped, and she sat there, stunned.

He continued. "I told you Angie and I were dating, but that wasn't true." He rushed on. "I didn't mean to lie, it just sort of happened. And then, once I'd said we had a good date, I didn't know how to take it back, so I said we were going out again."

Sidney knew he was pausing so she could say something, but no words would come out. Why was he telling her this? What did he expect her to say? She wrapped the quilt tighter around her.

"I'm sorry," he said. "If you're upset with me, I understand."

She was, but she couldn't tell him that. "No, you're fine. That's okay. I understand." The words sounded robotic, even to her ears.

He stared at her thoughtfully for a moment. "You okay? You never called me."

"Sorry." She looked to the polished, hardwood floor. "I've been busy." *Busy trying to push you out of my head.*

He glanced at the horror film paused on her TV. "You look real busy."

She blushed. "Just trying to de-stress."

"You have any popcorn? I could use some de-stressing."

She should say no. Shove him out the door. But looking in his blue eyes was weakening her resolve. "In the kitchen."

He stood and crossed the room. "I'll make the popcorn."

"Do you want me to re-start this movie, or pick a different one?" She was going to regret this.

"You choose." He walked into the kitchen and started rummaging through her cupboards.

"Second one on the right," she called.

"Found it," he called back.

Sidney picked up the remote and scrolled through the selections. When she came to *What's Up Doc,* she smiled. That was the one.

He came back in the room with a silver bowl. The smell made her mouth water. It had been a while since she'd made popcorn. It was difficult to eat a whole batch by herself.

Blake sat on the couch and she bit her lip, wondering if she could still sit in her chair and share the popcorn.

"Come on." Blake motioned to the seat next to him.

She decided not to argue with him and plopped down beside him. She covered herself with the quilt to add a little buffer. Then she started the movie.

He chuckled. "I haven't seen this in years."

"Me neither." She grinned up at him. "Remember how we used to watch this over and over? I think we wore out the tape."

"And we annoyed Natalie by repeating our favorite quotes."

She poked him in the side. "Don't hog the popcorn."

As they watched the movie, she curled up under the quilt. At some point, Blake must have gotten cold because halfway through the movie she realized he was under the quilt with her. Not a good thing, because by the end of the movie she was totally snuggling with him.

She looked up and her gaze connected with his. That was a mistake. All the feelings for Blake she'd been pushing away suddenly crashed down on her, and she wondered why he was here with her. Could it be possible he had some of the same feelings she did?

The thought startled her and she hopped up and grabbed the popcorn bowl. "That was fun." She went into the kitchen and stuck the bowl under the faucet.

Blake followed her. "It was."

He looked serious, and her heart pounded. Could he really be spending time with her because he wanted something more? The implications swirled in her head as her hands shook. Maybe he told her about Angie because he hoped to start up a relationship with her. She squirted a little soap on the popcorn bowl and grabbed a washcloth, deep in thought.

Blake hooked his thumbs in his jeans. "So, I wanted to apologize again for lying. I honestly didn't mean to."

She shrugged her shoulders, unsure of where he was going with it. She rinsed the bowl and grabbed a dishtowel.

"Has that kind of thing ever happened to you before?"

She froze. "What?"

"You know." He avoided eye contact. "Maybe you didn't mean to lie about something, but it happened and you didn't know how to come clean."

Grayson. He'd told Blake about her fake engagement. Anger and embarrassment coursed through her. How could he have done that? She dried the bowl then set it down on the counter. "Nope." She challenged him with a stare.

He blew out a breath and raised his hands. "All right. I tried everything. I give up."

She narrowed her eyes at him. "What are you talking about?"

"I know you weren't really engaged to Ted."

"I can't believe Grayson told you!" She tossed the dish-towel on the sink and huffed out of the room.

"Grayson didn't say anything."

Blake's voice was right behind her and she turned to face him. "Then who?"

He balked, and took a step back. "It doesn't matter. What matters is, I've known for weeks, and I've given you every opportunity to tell me. I thought if we spent more time together, you'd feel more comfortable talking to me. So, I took you to the lake. I came over. We talked. I've told you things I've never told anyone else." His voice rose. "But no matter what I do, you lie to me." His eyes shot accusing daggers at her.

Her mouth dropped open. He'd known this whole time? That's why he'd been coming around? And that's why he told her about Angie? It wasn't because he had feelings for her?

Humiliation filled her and her neck burned. Once again, Blake was making her feel like nothing. Less than nothing. He'd made her open up her heart to him, and all he wanted was to see if he could make her crack.

She clenched her hands into fists. "Get out."

He folded his arms. "Right. You're mad at me. Because *you* lied."

"Get. Out." She pointed to the door, too livid to do anything else.

"Fine. I'll go. I just want to know one thing." He paused. "Why?"

Because I didn't want to fall back in love with you. The words echoed in her head. Her heart thumped loudly in her ears. Too late. She took a step away from him. "I want you to leave. Now."

His shoulders fell and he walked to the door. He opened it but didn't leave. He turned to her. "Listen, I'm sorry. I didn't mean—"

"Stop." Sidney was in no mood to talk about it anymore. All she wanted to do was crawl into bed and forget about the last few weeks of her life. Her stomach burned with acid, and she couldn't breathe. She closed her eyes, hiding the moisture that was building up, threatening to make the situation even more humiliating. "Just leave. And don't come back."

The door shut and she opened her eyes.

Blake was gone.

~

Blake slid behind the wheel of his truck and stared at Sidney's apartment door. Why had he confronted her with the truth? Of all the stupid things he could have done, that was the worst. He had spent the week wondering why she'd broken off her pretend engagement. In all honesty, he was hoping it was because she wanted to make herself available to him.

But that obviously wasn't the reason. She was continuing to distance herself from him, even after he'd gotten her to let down her guard tonight. His bright idea of telling her the truth about Angie in the hopes that it would give her a way to come clean about Ted hadn't worked at all. She would have held onto that lie forever.

His only choice, he'd thought, was to tell her he knew. Big mistake. Now she was not only holding him at arm's length, she was tossing him out the door. He hit his steering wheel with the palm of his hand. She might never speak to him again. And for what? Because he couldn't let her lie go? Stupid.

Was it his pride that wouldn't let it go, or something else? Why was he so hung up on her? And then it hit him.

He was in love with Sidney.

He loved the way she laughed, and the way he felt when she was around. She completed him. And he wanted her to come clean about Ted because that would mean she trusted him fully.

He needed that trust after his last failed relationship. But for some reason, she didn't want to give it to him. She pushed him away. And instead of waiting for her trust, he had forced the issue. Now she hated him.

He started his truck and drove out of her parking lot, his stomach in knots. He might have just blown his chance at any kind of relationship with Sidney.

~

Sidney spent the rest of the weekend trying to forget about the whole Blake fiasco. Her heart couldn't take any more Blake, so she deleted his profile out of her computer. She threw out the Monopoly game he'd left at her apartment and deleted him from her phone.

The official Blake purge was underway. She threw away the materials she'd gotten from her skydiving instruction class. She even tossed the calendar where she'd written the event in red. If she could bleach her brain to forget the last few weeks, she'd do it in a heartbeat.

Then, after taking the trash out to the dumpster, she sat in her living room and stared at the wall. An image of Blake's face popped into her head, unwanted. He had the bluest eyes. His smile could melt her heart in seconds.

She loved him, and he would never see her as worthy of his affections.

A tear escaped, and she quickly brushed it off her cheek. No. She did not want to waste her time crying over Blake. She needed to cut him from her life and move on.

CHAPTER 23

Sidney glanced at the clock. Almost five. Ten more minutes and she'd be able to close up shop and go home to the frozen dinner awaiting her. She sighed. It had been a month since she'd last seen Blake. A month of dead silence. He hadn't texted, called, or come over. That was what she wanted, though, right?

It was what she had thought she wanted. She'd thought that if she didn't see him, didn't speak to him, the painful hole in her chest would close up and she'd be able to move on. Instead, the hole seemed to grow, and nothing she did filled it.

She opened up her social media accounts and posted something about being glad it was almost the weekend. Thursday wasn't as good as Friday, but at least it was coming. Her phone pinged and she checked the message.

Phyllis: *Did you hear? Blake's mother passed away this morning.*

Sidney's breath caught, and her hands began to shake. He hadn't called her. She shook her head. Of course he hadn't. She'd told him not to contact her. And now she felt awful.

Sidney: *Oh, no! How?*

Phyllis: *Brain aneurism. She went suddenly.*

Blake.

He must be in so much pain. She grabbed her purse and headed out, locking her door and jumping in her car. Before she had time to think about it, she pulled up in front of his house. His truck sat in the driveway.

She ran up the walkway and rang his doorbell. When he answered the door, his hair disheveled and red rims under his eyes, she felt even worse. "Blake." She didn't wait for him to say anything. She rushed to him and enveloped him in her arms.

He held her in a crushing hug. A choking sob escaped him, and she clung to him even tighter. "I'm so sorry," she said, a tear escaping down her cheek.

After a moment, he pulled back, his emotions in check. He motioned for her to come inside, and she entered his living room. She didn't know what to say, so she waited for him to speak.

"Do you want anything to drink?" he asked, his voice raspy.

She shook her head no.

He motioned to the couch. "Would you like to sit?"

She sat on his couch and folded her legs under her. She felt so bad about the way she'd treated him the last time they'd spoken, and yet, she had no idea what to say to make it right.

He sat next to her. "Thank you for coming. Means a lot to me."

"Are you okay?"

He nodded. "I just…it came as a shock."

"I know." She placed her hand on his, and then immediately regretted it as the tingles started up her arm. She resisted the urge to pull away. She was there to comfort him.

He took her hand in his and gently squeezed, which sent her heart into overdrive. "She lived her life to the fullest. I can be happy about that."

"And she was glad you were close, I'm sure."

"Yes." A sad smile appeared on his face. "I should have moved back sooner. I could have done my residency here."

"Don't do that. You couldn't have known."

He rubbed his forehead and sighed. "You're right." He stood, letting go of her hand. "Can we go for a walk? I need to get out of here."

"Sure."

They started down the sidewalk in the quiet residential neighborhood. Sidney wasn't sure what to say, but she knew Blake needed her there, so she walked alongside him in silence.

"You know, every year she would ask me what I wanted for my birthday dinner. It was always the same, macaroni and cheese. She hated macaroni and cheese, but she made it, every year."

"She was a good mother."

He smiled, but it didn't reach his eyes. "She was sick a lot when I was young, but she always made me my birthday dinner."

Sidney patted him on the shoulder.

"I remember one Christmas I had my heart set on getting a Nintendo 64. I was twelve. Stores for miles were sold out. I heard on the news that stores were taking orders, but they weren't going to be filled for months. I was heartbroken."

A light breeze blew the scent of a lilac bush over the air. She turned to him. "What happened?"

He chuckled. "Somehow, my mother pulled it off. It was there under the tree on Christmas morning. I was so excited, I screamed loud enough they probably heard me in Japan."

She laughed. "What did she do, mug someone?"

"I have no idea. She would never tell me." He grew serious. "She loved Christmas. It was her favorite time of year."

As they walked, the sun dipped lower in the sky. Long shadows stretched across the sidewalk. Blake told her stories about his mother, and she listened. She knew he needed to talk.

They walked until it got dark. When they got back to Blake's house, Sidney was famished. "How about I make us something to eat?"

Blake sat down on the couch. "Thank you. I haven't eaten all day."

She rummaged through the cupboards and managed to throw together a dinner with salad, some pasta, and some grilled chicken. She went into the living room to tell Blake the dinner was ready, and found him asleep.

Her heart went out to him. He had been exhausted. She covered his plate and put it in the fridge, then found a blanket in the closet. She tucked it around him, then ate her dinner alone. When she was done, she rinsed her plate and quietly left his house.

She didn't see Blake again until the funeral. He sat in the front row of the chapel beside his aunt and uncle, and their children. Sidney slipped into a seat several rows back. The music filled the chapel and Sidney tried to hold it together. It was tearing her apart not being able to hold Blake's hand and comfort him.

After the service, she slipped out the back door and crossed the parking lot. She didn't want to stay for the luncheon. As she climbed into her car, she saw Blake step out and stop by the door. He stood and watched her pull out of the parking lot.

CHAPTER 24

Sidney tied her running shoes. It had been three weeks since the funeral, and she hadn't heard from Blake. She figured she wouldn't. It didn't lessen the pain any, though.

She strapped her phone to her arm and started her playlist, but instead of her favorite pop song, *Stairway to Heave*n started playing. Heaviness settled in her chest. Instead of changing it, she let the classic rock song play as she jogged down her street.

She'd heard the song before, but she now listened to it with a new purpose. She wanted to understand the song. Wanted to pull the music into herself, and thus pull a little bit of Blake in as well. The melody was a bit haunting, but it went well with the lyrics, which spoke to her about the focus on material things in this life. She thought about Blake's ex-wife, and wondered if the song ever made him sad.

And then the song changed, grew more up-tempo, and she realized she was enjoying it. She listened to it three times before she let the playlist go on to the next classic rock song. *Hotel California*. She let the rest of the music play as she ran.

Listening to Blake's music made her feel closer to him, even though it magnified the pain. She no longer cared about that. It was obvious she wouldn't outlive the hollow feeling inside her.

She got back to her apartment and stepped into the shower, playing the rest of Blake's playlist on her Bluetooth speaker. She longed for the time she'd spent with him. The times they would talk, or just goof around. The way he smiled, and the way he always knew what to say to make things better. She missed him.

The shampoo lathered in her hair as she listened to *Don't Stop Believin'* and wondered what Blake was doing today. Maybe she couldn't have him the way she wanted to, but avoiding him was ripping her apart.

She turned off the water. What would he do if she showed up at his house, like he used to at hers? Would he hang out with her? Seemed to her that he was okay being friends. Maybe just being friends was better than this pain of not being around him anymore. The realization of this rocked her, and she decided to drive over to Blake's house after she got dressed. She grabbed her Scrabble game on the way out the door.

Blake pulled the door open and his eyebrows rose when he saw her. "Hi."

She ignored the 'what are you doing here' look on his face. "I came for a rematch," she said, throwing his own words back at him and holding up the board game.

His lips twitched, but he didn't smile. "I'd love to, but I'm kind of in the middle of something."

She tried not to let her disappointment show. "What are you doing?"

"Packing."

Her heart pounded in her chest. "Going on a trip?"

"No, I uh…" He rubbed his forehead. "I'm moving."

Time slowed. Her throat constricted and she couldn't speak. Blake was leaving. Again. "Where?" she said, her voice barely above a whisper.

"To Minnesota. I got a job offer…and well, with Mom gone, I just felt like it was time to move on."

Because there's nothing left for you here. She swallowed. "I see."

He stepped back. "Do you want to come in for a minute? I have some Coke in the fridge. That's about all I have."

Too stunned to think clearly, she nodded and stepped inside. The moment he shut the door, she wondered what she was doing there. He clearly didn't think of her as anything important in his life. And just to prove it, he was leaving. For good this time.

She didn't know what to say or do. She simply followed him into the kitchen and side stepped the boxes as he grabbed a can of Coke. He held it out to her. "Sorry, I packed the glasses already."

"When are you leaving?" she blurted out.

"In the morning."

She opened the can and took a sip. Being used to drinking diet, she didn't expect the drink to be so sugary. She set the can down on the counter. "Do you need any help?" Gah, why ask him that? She should leave. Now. Because any second now the tears would come and she didn't want Blake to be standing right there when they started to fall.

He seemed surprised she offered, but he smiled. "Sure." He led her to his bedroom closet, where he was packing the last of his clothes. A few boxes lay scattered around on the floor.

She noticed an open box full of papers near the wall. She didn't mean to snoop, but she couldn't help seeing what lay on top. She reached in and pulled out an old school photo of hers. She'd written on the back, 'To Blake. Love, Sidney.'

"Oh, this is nice. Me, at that awkward stage." She mimicked the awful cringe of a smile of hers at the age of thirteen.

He reached out and snatched the photo from her, smiling. "I like that picture."

"What else do you have in here, anyway?" she asked, crouching and peeking in the box.

"Just personal stuff." He laughed and tried to close the flaps.

Even more curious now that he was trying to hide it, she grabbed the box away from him. "Let's see," she said, looking inside. "What is this?" She pulled out an old school paper.

He reached for it, but she pulled it away. She read in childhood handwriting, "When I grow up, I'm going to invent a machine that will make ice cream sandwiches. It will make so many I will give them to all the kids so no one will be sad."

She giggled. "Aw, that's cute."

He blushed and took the paper from her.

She looked in the box again. "You saved all your old school stuff?" She grinned up at him. "Are you a closet pack rat?"

"It's just one box."

She reached in and pulled out another photo of her. This time it was her senior picture. She stared at it. Blake had been away at college. She hadn't given him her senior photo. This had been taken during the time when he wasn't talking to her. "Where did you get this?" Her voice was so low, it almost came out as a whisper.

He shrugged. "I think Grayson sent it to me." He took the box from her and stuck his hand out for the photo.

She handed it to him, silent.

He slipped the photo into the box and folded the flaps. "If you want to finish taking the clothes from the hangers, you can fold them and put them in that garment box." He pointed.

She nodded, too stunned to say anything.

~

Blake taped the box and put it on a stack in the living room. What was Sidney doing? Why had she shown up now, of all times? He'd pretty much accepted that she was never going to trust him. Never give him what he truly wanted. Herself.

Maybe she'd been too burned by Asher. Maybe she'd grown too jaded. He wasn't sure, but she'd been running from him ever since he stepped into her business and hired her. She had made her intentions clear. They were friends, and that was it.

Being in Bishop Falls was too hard on him, with Sidney so close and yet unavailable to him, so he'd sent out his resume. It hadn't taken long before he had a job offer. He'd accepted the first one.

And now Sidney was here, making him re-think his decision to leave. Every time she was around, all he wanted to do was pull her into his arms. The smell of her hair made him replay their kiss in his head. Being near her was both torture and sweet happiness, and he wasn't sure he wanted to give up that small piece of heaven.

What was he thinking? He couldn't stay. He needed to leave and forget about the way she made him feel…like he was falling from the plane again.

No.

Falling in love.

Yes, he knew it now. He was in love with Sidney. And that was why he had to leave. Because being in love with someone who didn't love you back was like...like his marriage to Melody. Full of pain.

He sighed and went back into his bedroom. Sidney was folding his shirts and placing them neatly in his garment box. His suitcase sat on the floor by his bed. She glanced up at him. "The closet is almost done."

"Thanks."

"What do you want to do next?"

"The only thing left to pack is under the bathroom sink." He went to find a good sized box for that.

When they were done packing the bathroom, he stood and stretched. "Do you want to go to lunch?"

She bit her lip like she wasn't sure she wanted to, but then nodded. "Okay."

They went outside. He opened the passenger door for her and she climbed in his truck. After he started the engine, she flipped on the radio, then looked at him with one eyebrow raised. "You've been listening to the pop station?"

Oh. Busted. He tried to play it cool and shrugged. "It's been growing on me."

She laughed and he realized he wouldn't get to hear that sound again after today. He clenched his jaw. He needed to get a grip.

After lunch, he went and picked up the moving truck. Sidney helped him haul all his boxes onto the truck. When only the heavy stuff was left, he turned to her. "I've got some guys coming over in the morning to help with the rest."

She nodded. "Okay, then." She ran her hand through her hair and looked toward her car. She was about to leave.

His heart climbed into his throat. The urge to pull her close and kiss her almost overwhelmed him, but he took a step back. It wouldn't be right. He'd never be able to tell her how he felt.

She swallowed and blinked up at him. "I guess I'll go."

He couldn't hold back any longer, and he pulled her into a hug. He held onto her for what seemed to be like a longer than acceptable time, but she didn't squirm to get away. She simply let him hug her.

When he pulled back, she had tears in her eyes. Surprised, he wiped one with his thumb. "Why are you crying?"

She laughed a little and stepped back from him. "Stupid, right? I mean, I'm sure we'll see each other. It's not like... you're never coming back."

He wasn't sure what to say. He certainly didn't plan on coming back to Bishop Falls. His plan was to move away and bury the pain...until maybe someday he'd be able to skydive again without remembering the way she felt in his arms. Or get up in the morning without wondering what she was doing at that moment. He nodded, a numb feeling overtaking him. "Right."

She backed up. "This isn't goodbye then. It's see you later."

"See you, Sidney."

She turned and walked toward her car. She paused, like she wanted to turn and say something, but she must have changed her mind because she started walking again. She got in her car, and he watched her drive out of his life. For good.

CHAPTER 25

Sidney tossed and turned all night, unable to shake the feeling that she'd made the biggest mistake of her life. Blake was leaving, and she hadn't told him the truth. Not really. He'd found out about her lie, but not the reason behind it.

She loved him. And he was leaving. She rolled over and punched her pillow. Would it make a difference if she told him? There were times when she wondered. When he held her and she thought maybe he could feel it too. And then other times she wasn't sure.

Time slowed and she lay there, thinking about Blake. He'd kept her school photo all these years. Did that mean something? He'd also kept that paper he'd written, so it might mean nothing. She wished she knew how he felt about her.

When sleep didn't return, she finally got out of bed at five o'clock and took a shower. The warm water felt good on her back and she stood there, wondering if she was crazy.

What if she did tell him? If he left anyway, all she'd have would be one more embarrassing incident. She'd handled those before. One more wouldn't kill her. But what if she told him and he decided to stay in Bishop Falls? What if her love for him was enough?

She turned off the faucet and wrapped herself in a towel. If she didn't tell him, he'd leave for certain. So, her only choice was to go over there and spill her guts, right? If she had any chance with him, she had to know. It was now or never.

Making the decision gave her both relief, and major butterflies. She dressed and tried to eat something, but her stomach wouldn't let her. She looked at the clock. Six-fifteen. She couldn't go over there this early. She plopped down on her couch and picked up her romance novel. She'd never finished it. Might as well.

Sidney wasn't aware that she'd fallen asleep until the noise of a truck outside brought her back to consciousness. A sick feeling filled her chest and she sprang up from the couch. What time was it? She ran to the clock. Ten!

She raced to the bathroom and ran a brush through her hair. She hadn't meant to fall asleep! Blake could be gone by now.

She ran to her car and hopped in. Her fingers shook as she turned the ignition. He was gone, she was certain. She had to stop for a red light and her heart pounded. She wasn't going to make it, was she?

He just had his bed and a few other things to load up. Surely he was done with that by now. She pressed the gas as soon as the light turned green. When she turned onto his street, she craned her neck to see if the big moving truck was still in front of his house.

She didn't see it.

No, no, no. The word echoed in her head as she drew closer. He was already gone.

She stopped the car in front of his house, her heart torn

in two. No moving truck. No Blake. The house stood empty, mocking her.

She rested her forehead on the steering wheel, the hole in her chest threatening to open up and swallow her. She should have told him yesterday. Or better yet, she should never have lied to him in the first place.

Maybe she could do some Googling. Find out where in Minnesota he was. Maybe she could drive there…

A knock on her window startled her and she jumped. She looked up. Blake? Her heart pounded in her chest. He wasn't gone? She got out of her car, feeling a bit foolish.

"Sidney?" The question in his eyes said more than his words.

"I, uh, needed to tell you something." She leaned against her car and fiddled with her fingers, her heart in her throat.

"What?"

She didn't look him in the eye. "I…" She swallowed. "My computer came up with another match for you."

His eyebrows drew together. "Excuse me?"

"I know, it's weird, because I put your account on hold, but another match came up and I thought I'd better tell you about her. You see, I think she's perfect for you."

He blinked, then his lips twitched. "You do?"

She rushed ahead, sure that if she stopped, she wouldn't get the words out. "Yes. She's an outdoor girl, loves hiking, canoeing, and swimming. And get this…she loves to skydive."

He folded his arms across his chest, his eyes holding amusement. "Really?"

"And…not to brag or anything, but my matchmaking skills are top notch. I think you should meet this girl. Give her a chance."

"Maybe I will."

Her pulse raced and she twisted her hands. "I know this comes at a bad time…you moving and all…"

He placed his hands on her car, on either side of her, trapping her. "I canceled the move last night."

His voice was so low, she barely heard him. "You did?"

"Yes. The guys helped me move everything back inside this morning. So, maybe it's fate." His gaze traveled over her face. "When can I meet this match?"

"That's the best part. You already know her."

He was so close now she could smell the slight mint on his breath. "I do? Who is this girl?"

"Me," she whispered, her heart pounding so loud she was sure he heard it.

His lips touched hers, and she closed her eyes, her nerve endings exploding. He cradled her face as he kissed her, and she allowed herself to get lost in him. Her heart soared and when he finally broke away, she nearly cried with joy.

He stared at her, his face serious. "Why didn't you match me with this wonderful girl before?"

Her breath caught, and she forced the words out. "I'm so sorry I lied. I was frightened."

He blinked in surprise. "Of me?"

"No." She looked down. "Not really. I mean...I was afraid of you rejecting me again." Her humiliation came back, threatening to choke her, and a tear slid down her cheek.

"What are you talking about?" He didn't say it accusingly. He spoke gently, his words almost caressing her.

"When I was sixteen. And I kissed you."

Realization formed on his face, and he rubbed the backs of his fingers down her cheek. "Sidney, I didn't reject you. I didn't even realize I had feelings for you. Not until you kissed me." He looked into her eyes. "You awoke things in me I'd never felt for anyone. It scared me, because you were so young." He pressed his forehead against her own. "I shouldn't have kissed you like that."

Another tear escaped. “But you left, and didn’t come back.”

“I’m sorry. I was wrong to stay away from you.”

She blinked away more tears. “At first I didn’t want to see you. I was embarrassed about the kiss. But then, I started hoping we could just forget about it. Maybe go back to the way things were before. I waited for Christmas holiday, thinking surely you’d come see me then. But you didn’t. And you stayed away for the next holiday, and the next.”

“Oh, Sidney.” He pulled her into his arms. “I was afraid to see you. Afraid of what you would think of me.”

“I thought you were the most wonderful person in the world,” she said, quietly.

He looked into her eyes. “And now? What do you think of me?”

The blue depths sucked her in, and she smiled. “I’m not sure. I might need another kiss to figure it out.”

He smiled, let out a chuckle, and then obliged.

EPILOGUE

Sidney looked in the mirror as Mia tugged on her hair. "Ouch," Sidney said, frowning. "Are you almost done?"

"I still have to fasten the veil. Hold your horses."

"My horses have been holding for an hour now." She shot Mia a cheesy smile.

"Funny." Mia fussed with her hair a little more, then placed the veil on. After a few pins and some disgruntled looks, Mia pronounced her done.

Sidney stood, her heart pounding. She smoothed out the long white skirt and turned to the side. "Do I look okay?"

"Girl, you look more than okay. Blake is going to trip over himself when he sees you."

Natalie walked into the makeshift dressing room and gasped. "Oh honey, you look amazing." She pulled Sidney into an embrace. "You're such a lovely bride."

Sidney blinked back the moisture. "How's Mom doing?"

"Madder than a hornet's nest under water, but she'll get over it. It's your wedding. If you want to jump out of a plane, no one should stop you."

Sidney smiled and hugged her sister again. "You're the best."

Together, they walked through the small airport to the waiting area where her father stood. He smiled when he saw her. "My little girl."

She refrained from rolling her eyes. "All grown up, Daddy."

"You'll always be my little girl." He took her hand and placed it in the crook of his arm. "Are you ready to do this?"

"I've been ready practically my whole life."

He smiled. "I know. I'm just glad you two figured everything out."

They stood and waited until their cue, then her father opened the door. They walked outside and down the white fabric leading to the small airplane. The cameraman clicked as they walked, and she tried not to trip on her long dress. Her father helped her climb in the plane, where her family sat, buckled in. Ted was seated beside Natalie, and Mia and her husband were in the back. White flowers and organza bows decorated the small space. She joined Blake, who stood before Reverend Joseph.

Nerves shot through her as Reverend Joseph began the ceremony. She looked up into Blake's eyes, and she calmed. His gaze was so full of love, she could barely breathe. How could she be so lucky?

This man, whom she'd loved her whole life, was now looking at her in adoration. It was the way she used to look at him as they paddled across the lake or watched late night TV after her parents had gone to bed. She had always dreamed he would someday see her this way.

And now he did.

Her turn came to say her vows, and she blinked back tears. "Blake. You make my heart so full. I've loved you since the day you and Grayson babysat me and you made milk come out of my nose." She paused as everyone laughed. "You stepped into my life very early, but I always knew you were the one for me. Now, today, you're making me the happiest woman in the world. I promise to love, honor, and cherish you forever."

Blake smiled. "Sidney. You were always the bright spot in my day. You knew how to make me laugh and make me bend over backwards to make you happy." He paused for some chuckles. "Even when we were kids, I knew there was something special about you. And now, here you are, beside me, ready to embark on this new adventure together. My love for you has grown each day, and I can't wait to spend the rest of my life with you. I promise to never leave you, to love you more each day, and to enjoy my time with you as we grow old together."

Sidney's mother sniffed, and she gave her mom a smile. After a few more words and the 'I do's, Reverent Joseph pronounced them husband and wife. "You may kiss the bride."

Blake put his arms around her and pressed his lips to hers. Her heart almost burst from her chest. The kiss didn't last long, but she knew she'd remember it for the rest of her life.

Reverend Joseph congratulated them, then stepped off the plane. Blake grinned at her and grabbed the gear. "Ladies first."

She found the Velcro and unfastened her long flowing skirt, revealing the white pants she had on underneath. Her sister whooped as she put on her parachute. Over the past six months, she'd been taking lessons and could now make the jump on her own.

Blake handed her the helmet and goggles, then he slipped into his own gear. Once they were ready, they sat down and buckled their seatbelts for take-off. Blake reached over and took her hand. Tingles spread up her arm. "You're not scared, are you?"

She grinned at him. "The scary part's over."

He pretended to sock her in the arm. "You're too funny."

When the plane reached altitude, Ted hopped up out of his seat. "Before you two jump, I have a special musical number for you."

Blake turned to her, his eyebrows up. "Did you know about this?"

"I admit nothing." She pressed her lips together and tried not to smile.

Ted pulled out a karaoke machine and a microphone. He, of course, was wearing a white shirt and tie. Sidney wasn't sure she'd ever seen him in anything else. He pressed a button and the opening of "Somebody to Love" by Queen rang out.

Ted started singing, and Sidney was surprised to find he could really sing. He belted out the song, really hamming it up as much as he could in the confined space. When he finished, the plane erupted in applause.

Then it was time for the jump. Sidney put on her goggles and adjusted her helmet. Blake finished adjusting his straps and stood beside her. She clasped his hand, ready to take the leap of her life.

He counted down and they jumped together, still holding hands. The wind whipped her hair as she and Blake free fell for a while, then they let go and Blake maneuvered away from her a bit so they could pull their parachutes.

The feeling of falling was amazing, and she once again experienced that rush of adrenalin and emotion. She got dizzy as she spun, but she loved the feeling. After they both pulled their cords, she looked over at her husband. A surge of love overwhelmed her, and she had to blink back tears.

He was everything she ever wanted. All her life, she'd

loved him, and now they were married. She could hardly believe it.

The earth grew larger as she neared, and she prepared for landing. She was the first to touch down, but Blake landed only moments after her, a few yards away. She removed her goggles and helmet and ran to him.

He leaned over and gave her a kiss, then threaded his arm around her and they walked toward her car in the parking lot.

Mia had tied tin cans to the back, and where it used to say Blissfully Matched, she'd crossed out the word 'matched' so it now read Blissfully Married.

Sidney smiled, thinking nothing was more appropriate.

He smiled at her. "How do you feel, Mrs. Wellington?"

"Like I could fly."

The End

AFTERWORD

Thank you for reading! If you like Victorine's books, check out her bundles she has on sale on her website. You can save big with a bundle! Use the code 20OFF and get 20% off your entire order!

www.victorinelieske.com

If you want to read what Victorine is writing as she writes it, check out her Patreon. For just a few bucks a month you can get early access to her stories!: https://www.patreon.com/Victorine

Join Victorine's Newsletter and get a free novella: Her Sister's Fiancé. https://BookHip.com/CXNTMH

VICTORINE'S T-SHIRT SHOP

Sometimes the characters in Victorine's novels wear funny t-shirts. If you like them, you can buy them at Victorine's T-shirt shop.

And it's not just T-shirts, Victorine has cloth masks, mugs, and other merchandise. They're fun! Take a peek!

https://victorinelieske.threadless.com/

ABOUT THE AUTHOR

Victorine and her husband live in Nebraska with their four children and two cats. She loves all things romance, and is currently addicted to Korean Dramas, which are super swoony and romantic. (She highly recommends Crash Landing on You on Netflix.)
When she's not writing, she's designing book covers for authors or making something with her extensive yarn collection.